**Welcome to the world
of Sydney Harbour Hospital
(or *SHH*…for short—
because secrets never stay hidden for long!)**

Looking out over cosmopolitan Sydney Harbour, Australia's premier teaching hospital is a hive of round-the-clock activity—with a *very* active hospital grapevine.

With the most renowned (and gorgeous!) doctors in Sydney working side by side, professional and sensual tensions run sky-high—there's *always* plenty of romantic rumours to gossip about…

Who's been kissing who in the on-call room? What's going on between legendary heart surgeon Finn Kennedy and tough-talking A&E doctor Evie Lockheart? And what's wrong with Finn?

Find out in this enthralling new eight-book continuity from Mills & Boon® Medical™ Romance—indulge yourself with eight helpings of romance, emotion and gripping medical drama!

Sydney Harbour Hospital
From saving lives to sizzling seduction, these doctors are the very best!

Dear Reader

I hope you've been enjoying the *Sydney Harbour Hospital* continuity so far.

When I was asked to take part in this fabulous series I was thrilled to learn that I would be amongst seven other amazing Down Under authors helping to create this very special world and decorate it with real-life heros and heroines who are as dedicated to their work as they are to each other.

Being so far away from the rest of the world, I believe those of us in this little corner of the southern hemisphere bring a unique voice to the Medical line and to romance fiction as a whole. I am honoured to be counted amongst this number, and am so excited about the unfolding stories throughout this series.

In Book Three we see Luca and Mia, two ER docs whose potent sexual chemistry draws them together despite their better judgement. And it makes walking away harder than they ever imagined. I hope you enjoy their story and continue on to read the next five books.

The Sydney Harbour Hospital may be fictitious, but with its views over the sparkling harbour and the famous sails of the Opera House it's the perfect backdrop for all our couples to fall in love.

I hope you'll agree.

Love

Amy

SYDNEY HARBOUR HOSPITAL: HOSPITAL: LUCA'S BAD GIRL

BY
AMY ANDREWS

To six Aussies and a Kiwi—thank you!
I had so much fun writing this continuity with you. And to
Meredith Webber, an amazing writer, fabulous mentor and
generous friend. Your down-to-earth advice always keeps me
grounded and your encouragement has led me into new worlds.

First published in Great Britain 2012
by Mills & Boon, an imprint of Harlequin (UK) Limited.
Harlequin (UK) Limited, Eton House, 18-24 Paradise Road,
Richmond, Surrey TW9 1SR

© Harlequin Books S.A. 2012

Special thanks and acknowledgement are given to Alison Ahearn
for her contribution to the *Sydney Harbour Hospital* series

ISBN: 978 0 263 22691 1

Harlequin (UK) policy is to use papers that are natural, renewable and recyclable products and made from wood grown in sustainable forests. The logging and manufacturing process conform to the legal environmental regulations of the country of origin.

Printed and bound in Great Britain
by CPI Antony Rowe, Chippenham, Wiltshire

Amy Andrews has always loved writing, and still can't quite believe that she gets to do it for a living. Creating wonderful heroines and gorgeous heroes and telling their stories is an amazing way to pass the day. Sometimes they don't always act as she'd like them to—but then neither do her kids, so she's kind of used to it. Amy lives in the very beautiful Samford Valley, with her husband and aforementioned children, along with six brown chooks and two black dogs. She loves to hear from her readers. Drop her a line at www.amyandrews.com.au

Recent titles by the same author:

WAKING UP WITH DR OFF-LIMITS
JUST ONE LAST NIGHT…
RESCUED BY THE DREAMY DOC
VALENTINO'S PREGNANCY BOMBSHELL
ALESSANDRO AND THE CHEERY NANNY

**These books are also available in eBook format
from www.millsandboon.co.uk**

Sydney Harbour Hospital

Sexy surgeons, dedicated doctors,
scandalous secrets, on-call dramas...

Welcome to the world of Sydney Harbour Hospital
(or *SHH*...for short—because secrets never stay hidden for long!)

Last month new nurse Lily got caught up in the hot-bed of hospital
gossip in **SYDNEY HARBOUR HOSPITAL: LILY'S SCANDAL**
by Marion Lennox

Then gorgeous paediatrician Teo
comes to single mum Zoe's rescue in
SYDNEY HARBOUR HOSPITAL: ZOE'S BABY
by Alison Roberts

This month sexy Sicilian playboy Luca finally meets his match
SYDNEY HARBOUR HOSPITAL: LUCA'S BAD GIRL
by Amy Andrews

Then in April Hayley opens Tom's eyes to love in
SYDNEY HARBOUR HOSPITAL: TOM'S REDEMPTION
by Fiona Lowe

Join heiress Lexi as she learns to put the past behind her in May...
SYDNEY HARBOUR HOSPITAL: LEXI'S SECRET
by Melanie Milburne

In June adventurer Charlie helps shy Bella fulfil her dreams—
and find love on the way!
SYDNEY HARBOUR HOSPITAL: BELLA'S WISHLIST
by Emily Forbes

Then single mum Emily gives no-strings-attached surgeon Marco
a reason to stay in July
SYDNEY HARBOUR HOSPITAL: MARCO'S TEMPTATION
by Fiona McArthur

And finally join us in August as Ava and James
realise their marriage really is worth saving in
SYDNEY HARBOUR HOSPITAL: AVA'S RE-AWAKENING
by Carol Marinelli

And not forgetting Sydney Harbour Hospital's legendary heart surgeon
Finn Kennedy. This brooding maverick keeps his women on hospital
rotation... But can new doc Evie Lockheart unlock the secrets to his
guarded heart? Find out in this enthralling new eight-book continuity
from Medical™ Romance.

A collection impossible to resist!

These books are also available in ebook format
from www.millsandboon.co.uk

CHAPTER ONE

D*r* M*ia* M*c*K*enzie* didn't know it yet but her night was about to go from bad to worse.

And that was no mean feat.

A full moon didn't usually bode well for emergency departments and this clear, cold Saturday night was no different. Moonbeams sprinkled like fairy dust on the world-renowned surface of Sydney Harbour, lending a deceptive calm to the view from the windows of Sydney Harbour Hospital.

But inside the walls of the emergency department it was crazy town!

At two in the morning there had been no let up from the insanity. SHH, or The Harbour to those who worked there, was living up to its reputation as the busiest emergency department in the city.

'I could have been a dermatologist,' Mia grumbled to Dr Evie Lockheart, her best friend and flatmate, as she strode out of the resus cubical, turning her back on the torrent of abuse from a drug addict she'd just brought back from the brink of death.

'They don't get abused by patients at half past stupid o'clock. You know why? Because they're sleeping. No on-call, no such thing as a dermatological emergency in the middle of the night, no urgent consults required.'

Evie, clutching a portable ultrasound unit, grinned. 'You'd be bored to tears.'

Mia's long blonde ponytail swished against her shoulder blades as she made her way to the central nurses' station with the patient's chart in hand. 'I could do bored.'

Evie snorted. 'Yep, whatever you say.'

Mia ignored her friend's sarcasm. 'How much longer are you and George Clooney going to be with the MVA?'

Evie laughed. 'The name is Luca. Dr Luca di Angelo.'

As far as Mia was concerned, the hospital's new director of trauma looked more like the devil than an angel.

He certainly seemed to be having a devil of a time with every available female walking the halls of SHH in the very short time he'd been here.

Which was fine by her. It was his life. And in a way she admired him for it. She too liked to keep her liaisons short and sweet.

But maybe that's what caused an itch up her spine whenever he was around—besides his disturbing good looks apparently honed beneath a Sicilian sun. She recognised a kindred spirit.

And didn't like what she saw.

'And he really is quite dishy.'

'Yes,' Mia mused. 'That he is.'

Evie grinned. Now, why couldn't she be interested in a tall, dark, handsome Italian who was living up to the reputation of sex god that had preceded his arrival at The Harbour a few weeks ago? Why was it the infuriating, dictatorial Dr Finn Kennedy that her brain insisted on conjuring up with monotonous regularity?

'Anyway,' she said shaking the thought away. 'We're stabilising the patient at the moment. He needs to go to Theatre for a laparotomy.'

Mia nodded. 'Okay, but when he's gone, go home. You were supposed to have finished three hours ago.'

'Yeah, yeah.' Evie grinned as she departed.

Mia had ten minutes' respite to catch up on some charts before a stocky man with swarthy features and wild eyes burst through the ambulance bay doors. 'My wife…she's in labour. The baby's coming now!' And then turned around and raced out the door again.

Mia sprang to her feet as a shot of adrenaline surged into her system. She hurried after the man, followed by Caroline, the triage nurse. She didn't notice the chill in the air, just the beaten-up old car parked at a crazy angle near the doors and a woman's urgent cries.

'Hurry,' the man yelled, wringing his hands.

Mia was there in seconds. The woman was lying on the back seat yelling, 'It's coming, it's coming.'

'Hi, I'm Dr McKenzie,' Mia said over the din. 'What's your name?'

'Rh-Rhiannon,' the woman panted.

Mia smiled at her encouragingly. 'How far along are you?'

'Thirty weeks, she's thirty weeks, all right?' the husband barked.

The man seemed hostile and had his wife's needs not been so urgent she'd have told him to back off. The last thing she needed right now while having to deliver a ten-week premature baby was a man with some kind of chip on his shoulder.

'Caroline, page the neonatology team, please,' Mia said quietly as she reached for the endless supply of gloves she had stashed in her pockets. 'And get Arthur to bring out a gurney.

'Okay, let's have a look here,' Mia said calmly.

The woman groaned again and it took Mia two seconds to identify a crowning head, despite the poor light. 'Right, well, you're absolutely correct, Rhiannon, this baby is coming.'

'I have to push,' Rhiannon yelled.

'That's fine.' Mia nodded, her heart bonging in her chest like the bells of a clock tower. 'I'm here to catch.'

Thirty seconds later the scrawny bawling infant slipped into Mia's waiting hands. 'You have a boy.' Mia grinned, laying the baby on the cloth seat and hoping that Caroline thought to bring back something warm to protect the newborn from the brisk air.

'Let me see it,' the father demanded.

But Caroline arrived, blocking his view as she handed Mia a pre-packaged emergency birth pack and some blankets fresh out of the blanket warmer. 'Neonates are doing an emergency intubation in Labour ward,' she said quietly. 'They'll get here as soon as they can.'

Mia nodded as she quickly laid the babe on a warm soft blanket, unwrapped the birth pack and efficiently clamped and cut the cord. She bundled the still crying baby up and handed him to Caroline.

'Get him into Resus so we can give him a proper check over, although his lungs seem pretty fine to me.'

Caroline laughed as she turned to go.

'Where are you taking it?' the father demanded.

'Inside,' Caroline said calmly. 'You can come too if you like.'

The father stalked after Caroline while Mia and Arthur helped Rhiannon onto the gurney. They covered her in warm blankets and pushed her inside to the resus cube next to her baby. The little boy was quiet now as he basked beneath the warm rays of a cot's overhead heater.

The father was pacing the cubicle when they arrived and seemed agitated. 'Red hair. It's got red hair,' the father growled at Rhiannon as he approached her with a sneer on his face.

'Oh, for crying out loud, Stan. Your grandfather had red hair.'

'Whose is it?' he demanded, rattling the rail of the gurney. 'Who's the father?'

Mia felt the hairs rise on the back of her neck as the father's puzzling behaviour gained some context. But context or not, he didn't get to act like a bully in her ER.

Thoughts of her own father wormed their way into her head and she quashed them ruthlessly.

'Sir!' Mia stood between him and the exhausted Rhiannon. 'You will not raise your voice in here. Whatever the issue is, this is not the time or place for it. Now, why don't you go and shift your car from the ambulance bay? When you come back, you'd better have calmed down or I *will* call Security.'

Mia was used to dealing with emotionally charged situations. Also drunks, drug addicts and a whole bunch of other people who didn't respect the sanctity of a hospital.

But she was a doctor. And Rhiannon and the baby were her patients. It was her duty to protect them.

The man scowled at her and left, muttering to himself.

'I'm sorry,' Rhiannon apologised. 'He gets so paranoid sometimes but he's harmless.'

Mia smiled. 'It's fine.'

A midwife from the maternity ward chose that moment to arrive. 'The team's going to be another twenty minutes or so,' she apologised.

'That's all right,' Mia dismissed. 'I think this little tyke's going to be fine.'

The ugly incident with Stan was forgotten as the midwife tended to Rhiannon, delivering the placenta while Mia gave the baby a check over. 'They'll probably want to keep him for the night in Special Care, given his early arrival, just to be on the safe side,' Mia pronounced, 'but everything checks out so far.'

She stood aside for the midwife to wrap the little boy up in that special way they did with babies so they looked just like glowworms, with only their little faces showing. Then Mia picked up the precious little package and asked, 'Would you like to hold your son?'

Rhiannon nodded and Mia was walking the baby over to her when the curtain flicked back a little and Stan stood there, looking slightly mollified. The time away seemed to have helped. Mia changed tack. 'Would you like to hold him?' she asked.

In Mia's experience, babies melted even the hardest of hearts. What man could resist such a gorgeous package? Hopefully this little impatient cherub would help Stan focus on what was important in life.

He looked uncertain for a moment then looked at Rhiannon. 'Can I?'

She smiled at him and Mia could see the love shining in the other woman's eyes. 'Of course.'

Mia eased the little bundle into Stan's arms. He seemed more dazed than elated but Mia knew that for some new fathers it was a big adjustment. He walked up and down the length of the cubicle with the baby, rocking him as he went, his gaze fixed on his face.

'What are you going to call him?' Caroline asked.

'I like Michael,' Rhiannon murmured.

The tight swaddling had loosened a little from the rocking and the baby stirred, displacing the wrap covering his head. Stan stopped as he stared down at a shock of red hair. He whipped around to face his wife. 'Is that his name?' he demanded. The baby started to cry. 'Michael? The man you've been sleeping with?'

Rhiannon groaned. 'Stop it, Stan. I'm sick of these accusations. You know there's only ever been you.'

'I want a paternity test,' he yelled.

Mia looked at Caroline then at a near-to-tears Rhiannon. 'Stan—'

Stan swung wildly around to face her and the baby cried louder. 'I want you...' he jabbed the air with an index finger '...to do a paternity test.'

'Stan this is ridiculous,' Rhiannon wailed, a tear trekking down her face.

Stan swung back. 'Are you refusing?'

'Okay, Stan, enough,' Mia said firmly. Stan turned abruptly and faced her. 'That is no way to be talking and certainly no way to be flinging a baby around. Listen to him, you're making him cry.'

She walked briskly towards Stan, her arms extended. 'Give him to me.'

Stan leapt back, his eyes wild again as he pulled a pocket knife out of his back pocket, flicking the blade open with one hand while he clutched his son in the other.

'Stay back,' he screamed. Caroline gasped, Rhiannon wailed and Mia stopped in her tracks. 'Don't come near me.'

Stan swung wildly from side to side, brandishing the knife as he backed slowly away from Mia.

Oh, good Lord! Mia felt a spurt of annoyance. *She did not have time for this.*

'Okay, Stan.' Mia summoned her most placatory voice as she put her hands out to calm the situation. She didn't think that Stan would harm anyone but that wasn't the way to play it when he was holding a brand-new thirty weeker in one arm and a knife in the other.

'Okay, I can do that for you,' she soothed, deftly placing her own body between Stan and Caroline.

Caroline, bless her cotton socks, picked up on her cue and quietly crept out of the cubicle. Mia knew one push of the panic button located under the desk in the nurses' station and every security guard rostered for the shift would be here in under two minutes.

'But you're going to need to give me the baby first.' She took another step towards Stan, tuning out the lusty newborn's cries and Rhiannon's pleading.

Stan slashed the blade through the air. 'No! Get back,' he yelled.

Luca di Angelo, who was passing the resus bay, frowned at the raised voice, louder even than the squalling baby. He strode in through the partially open curtain, surveying the scene rapidly.

A man with a knife. A bawling baby being held to ransom. A crying woman. A terrified nurse. And gutsy Dr Mia McKenzie—aloof, frosty little Mia—standing in the thick of it.

'What the devil is going on here?' he demanded.

Stan swung around again, slashing the air in Luca's general direction. 'Stay back,' he yelled.

Luca stopped. 'Dr McKenzie?'

'It's fine, Dr di Angelo,' she said, a placid smile plastered to her face as she inched closer to Stan. Very soon there'd be maximum force at her disposal—she could do without the Lone Ranger potentially ramping the situation up in the mean time.

Even if he did look good enough to spread on toast.

Mia's stomach rumbled.

'Stan here just wants a paternity test so he's going to give me the baby and I'll draw some blood. Right, Stan?'

'No.' Stan looked wildly between the two of them. 'The baby stays,' he insisted.

Luca watched Mia in his peripheral vision as she crept forward at a snail's pace. 'But how can we take blood when you're holding a baby, Stan?' Luca reasoned, distracting the man.

Mia, grateful if a little surprised that Luca had caught on really fast, took another step closer.

'Stay back,' Stan bellowed. The baby's cries rose another octave.

'I can't take your blood from here, Stan,' Mia soothed.

The adrenaline flowing through her system brought

everything into sharp focus. The sweat on Stan's brow. The harsh suck of his breath as he heaved air in and out of his lungs. The white spittle forming at the corner of his mouth. The way he turned the knife over and over in his palm and constantly shifted his weight from one foot to the other as his gaze darted between the two doctors.

But she was probably even more aware of Luca. Somehow it was he who dominated the room, not Stan. He towered over the knife-wielding man, all lean and broad shouldered, in sharp contrast to Stan's stocky stature. And despite the deceptive casualness of his hands-in-pocket stance, Mia could see the hard clench of his jaw and sense the coiled rigidity in those muscles barely contained behind the snug-fitting polo shirt.

She reminded him of a taipan, ready to strike. Swift and deadly.

Just then there was a commotion behind them as several security staff arrived at once.

Stan looked over Mia's shoulder. 'What are they doing here?' he roared, his hold on the baby tightening and causing further lusty protest.

Luca held out his hand as Stan's agitation increased. 'It's standard hospital procedure,' Luca soothed, moving a little closer. 'It'll be all right, though. I'm going to ask them to stand back, okay?'

'I don't think that's a good idea, Doc,' the chief security officer said.

'Back! You heard him, get back!' Stan shouted, brandishing the knife a little too close to the baby's head.

The midwife gasped.

Luca turned to the security contingent. 'It's okay,'

he assured them. Then he turned back to Stan. 'They're going, see?' Luca said as he heard the guards shuffling away.

Mia kept her gaze focused on Stan and the baby. 'Okay, Stan, now we've done something for you, you've got to do something for us.' She covered up her next step closer by holding out her arms. 'Give me the baby. He's scared and hungry. Listen to him. I'm sure a nice feed will settle him down and we can talk about this without upsetting him any more.'

And, frankly, the infant's cries were getting on her last nerve. The situation was fraught enough without the distinct urgency of an escalating newborn baby's cries.

'She's right, Stan,' Luca agreed as he edged nearer too. 'This isn't something a baby should be part of.'

'It's not my fault.' Stan's voice cracked as his face beseeched them. 'I work hard all day and she repays me by sleeping with half the neighbourhood.'

Mia felt a chill as if a ghostly hand from the past had stroked down her spine. She ignored it.

Luca nodded. 'I know. Believe me, I know.' And he did. He understood the desperation that Stan was feeling, the sense of betrayal. *Intimately.*

Mia glanced sharply at Luca. There was empathy, real empathy, in his tone.

'We can talk about all that, Stan,' Luca continued. 'Just give the baby to Dr McKenzie.'

Stan looked from one to the other and Mia saw the uncertainty on his face, saw that even Stan in his crazed state had registered Luca's compassion. She took advantage and moved forward slowly, unsurprised to sense Luca doing the same.

'It's okay, Stan, you're doing the right thing,' Mia reassured him.

Stan shook his head from side to side. 'I just need to know.'

'Of course,' Luca murmured. 'Of course you do, Stan.'

They were close now and Mia could sense Stan weakening. His grip on the knife had slackened. But so had his hold on the baby. Everything inside her urged her to leap forward and snatch the bawling infant from him but she knew any sudden movements would be a bad idea.

'Give your little boy to me, Stan,' she implored quietly.

Stan looked down at the crying bundle, the red hair even more vivid against the white of the wrap. He shook his head, his grip tightening again.

'He's not my baby!' he roared, lunging the knife at her.

Everything slowed as Mia watched it come towards her chest. She wasn't conscious of anything else, just the hypnotic arc of the blade as its point drew closer to her heart.

'Mia!'

Luca reached out and grabbed her, pulling her towards him. The sweeping slash of the knife missed her torso completely but sliced into the flesh of her upper arm. Mia gasped as bright, piercing pain stole her breath.

Luca swore in his native tongue as his hand shot out and crushed Stan's wrist in a vice-like grip. Stan yelped and dropped the knife.

'Security!'

His voice cracked like a whip into the charged atmosphere and in an instant five burly guards had entered the fray. The fight instantly went out of Stan at the sight of overwhelming force.

'The baby,' Luca demanded, and the midwife leapt forward, snatching the squalling infant.

'Go easy,' Luca ordered as the guards hauled a now passive Stan away. 'Are you okay?' he asked switching his attention to Mia.

She nodded automatically as the baby, now safe in his mother's embrace, began to settle. 'I'm fine.' Even though the hand that had instinctively covered the wound to apply pressure was sticky with her own blood. It had quickly oozed through the material of her cotton shirt.

Luca looked at the dark red blood running down her arm and shook his head. Most women he knew would have been hysterical by now. But not Mia. She'd kept her head in the face of an emotionally overwrought father with a knife and had dismissed what looked like a substantial wound as if it were a paper cut.

'Go to the minor ops room, I'll take a look at it.'

'It's fine, just superficial,' she said dismissively.

Luca pointed. 'Blood is running down your arm.'

Mia looked down at the thick trickle, surprised to see it. 'I'll get Evie to look at it.'

'I sent her home.'

'Dr di Angelo?' Caroline interrupted them. 'The psych reg is on the phone. He wants to speak with you.'

Luca quirked an eyebrow at her. 'I can't have one of my staff expiring from blood loss. It wouldn't look very good. Minor ops. Now. I'll be along after the call.'

Mia watched him go, a well of resentment rising in

her. She'd been looking after herself for a lot of years, she didn't need Mr Tall Dark and Handsome pulling the boss card and she certainly didn't need him fussing over her.

No one had ever fussed over her. *And that was just the way she liked it.*

A couple of steri-strips and she'd be fine.

A few minutes later, Mia pushed into the on-call room and plonked herself down at the table in the kitchen area, spilling her supplies on the cluttered top. Her arm hurt like hell and all she wanted to do was crawl into one of the private rooms off to her left and collapse on one of the pull-out beds.

The adrenaline had worn off and her earlier tiredness had taken hold and intensified.

And if she was asleep, the memories that Stan's actions had unleashed tonight couldn't bother her.

It was quiet in the room as she fumbled one-handed with the buttons of her blouse. The sleeves had a firm cuff that sat snugly around her biceps and couldn't be rolled up enough to gain a good visual of the damage. She winced as she slipped the blouse off, every movement jarring though her lacerated deltoid.

She tossed it on the floor—that was going straight in the bin.

She inspected her spaghetti-strapped top, pleased to see that no blood had seeped into it. This kind of undergarment was a permanent fixture beneath whatever shirt she was wore on a night shift. The hospital air-conditioning seemed to reach freezing point at around four in the morning and, even in summer, the extra layer helped.

Mia was especially grateful for it tonight.

She looked down at the wound on her upper arm. The blood had dried and crusted, making it difficult to tell the extent of the laceration. It looked ugly, though, as she gently probed it with her index finger. It was quite long and for a moment she let herself think about what could have happened had Luca not pulled her out of the way.

She noticed her hand was trembling and she dropped it from the wound, clamping down on her thoughts.

She hadn't been stabbed in the chest. She hadn't died. *Luca had pulled her out of the way.*

But it didn't stop the trembling from spreading to all her limbs and then to her insides. She took a couple of deep breaths, desperately trying to quell the outbreak.

It was a reaction, that was all. It would settle.

But the longer she sat, trying to get control of her breathing and the shaking, the more vulnerable she was to her emotions and thoughts. And she hated that—she'd learned long ago they didn't get you anywhere.

But tonight she didn't seem to be able to stop them.

Was that how her own father had felt when he'd found out about the paternity of her stillborn sister? Like Stan? Desperate and enraged? If there'd been a knife or a gun handy, would he have used it on her mother?

He'd walked away from them that day but she hadn't known why until years later. Years of blaming him for abandoning them, years of hating him, only to find out that it had been her mother's infidelities that had driven her father away.

Mia shook her head. *Stop it. Stop it!*

This situation tonight had come too close to home but there was no need to fall apart. She wasn't ten years old any more. She was an adult.

Clean yourself up and get back out there again!

Mia forced herself to action. To tend to the wound. Open the dressing pack, pour in some antiseptic lotion, pick up the gauze, work away at the dried blood.

It was awkward and hurt like the blazes but she welcomed the distraction from her thoughts and her shaking hands settled with a familiar routine.

Two minutes later Luca strode through the door. Mia glanced up at him, feeling strangely naked with her blouse discarded. Which was ridiculous—she was more than adequately covered. She ignored him, returning to the task at hand.

Luca lounged against the table and smiled to himself as Mia barely acknowledged his arrival. 'You're making a mess of that,' he mused.

Mia glared at him. 'It's a little difficult.'

'I do believe I told you I would attend to your wound.' He folded his arms across his chest. 'But you don't like asking for help, do you, little Mia?'

His slight accent gave his deep baritone a very sexy edge as it rolled over her. 'It's Mia, or Dr McKenzie. Please refrain from addressing me any other way.'

Luca chuckled as he pushed off the bench. 'Okay, *Mia.*' He sat on the chair next to her. 'Allow me,' he said as he picked up some gauze and dabbed at the wound.

Mia didn't protest—she was making a hash of it anyway. His touch was gentle as he coaxed the dried blood from the cut and she shivered. His fingers were dark against her paler skin and long.

Her father had long fingers. A pianist's hands. He was tall too, like Luca. He'd told her he was her prince and she was his princess and they'd be together for ever.

And then he'd left.

She squeezed her eyes shut. *Stop it. Stop it.*

Luca watched her. It was the first time he'd spent any length of time in her company and he was curious. He'd already noticed on their brief acquaintance she was a good-looking woman with a cute mouth and a sassy swagger.

But up close she was really quite exquisite.

Her face was long, as were her eyelashes. A frown appeared between her brows and her lips parted. She looked in pain.

'Am I hurting you?' he murmured.

Mia's eyes fluttered open. *How had he got that close?* She could see the individual whiskers making up the smooth blue-black of his jaw and just make out the black pupil in the middle of his bottomless brown eyes. His hair, as dark as his eyes, was thick with a slight wave that brushed his forehead and the tops of his ears.

And his mouth. The full curve to that bottom lip was wicked.

His fingers stroked gently over her skin as he cleaned the wound and it reminded her it had been a while since a man had touched her.

She lowered her gaze to the column of his throat. 'No.'

Luca was captivated by the slide show of emotions in her large blue eyes as magnificent and as transparent as a stained-glass window. The husky timbre of her voice wove between the bands of steel around his heart. 'Are you okay?'

Mia nodded, keeping her gaze firmly fixed on his throat. The long tanned column of his neck was also shaded in blue-black smoothness. She remembered how she'd loved the sandpaper roughness of her father's neck as he'd cuddled her close to read to her at night.

Damn it! She gripped the back of the chair hard. 'I'm fine.'

'You've been through an ordeal tonight. That knife came very close to—'

'I said I'm fine,' Mia interrupted, raising her face to scowl at him. 'Just clean the damn wound.'

CHAPTER TWO

LUCA paused in his ministrations for a moment, the blue of her eyes frosty now. He'd only known her for a few short weeks and while he'd been impressed with her empathy for patients and her good rapport with her colleagues he'd also sensed she was a woman who preferred to keep herself pretty much to herself.

But she'd always been polite about it.

Something was definitely eating at Mia McKenzie tonight.

He shifted his attention back to the wound.

'It's borderline,' he mused, looking at the clean ten-centimetre laceration. 'It's deeper laterally, could probably do with a couple of sutures there.'

Mia nodded to the pile of medical supplies on the table. 'Steri-strips there somewhere.'

'Sutures would be better.'

'Steri-strips will be fine.'

'The scarring will be worse if we use steri-strips.'

Mia shrugged. 'I don't care about a scar.'

Luca looked at her for a moment then fished around for the strips. 'Most women would,' he murmured when he located them. He doubted he'd ever been with a single woman who didn't obsess over the slightest blemish.

'I'm not most women.'

Luca chuckled. 'Yes. I think you are right.'

Mia sat still as he opened the packet and secured the wound edges together, applying firm tension through each sticky strip. Then he applied an adhesive dressing over the top. She watched as he absently brushed the pad of his thumb back and forth over the dressing as if he were a parent, rubbing a boo-boo better.

Just like her father had done.

'You look like you've got a lot on your mind,' he murmured.

Unfortunately, he was right. She hadn't been able to stop thinking about her father since Stan's episode. It had probably been the first time ever she'd been confronted with how emotionally untenable it had been for him to stay.

'It's busy,' she said brusquely, rising from the chair and clearing away the detritus from her dressing and tossing it in the bin. 'We can't just skulk in here all night.'

'The team have got it covered. And you're not going back out there until you've had a break. Try and get some sleep.' She opened her mouth to protest and he stood. 'That's an order.'

Great! What in the hell was she going to do alone in here with a bunch of unwanted memories that wouldn't quit? *Things she just wanted to forget.*

'What if a bus crash comes in?'

Luca grinned. 'I'll come and wake you.'

Mia felt the grin right down to her toes. It twinkled

in his eyes and gave the devil a whole new degree of wicked.

The fact that she noticed his twinkling eyes rankled. 'Are you flirting with me?' she demanded, crossing her arms.

Luca chuckled. She didn't beat around the bush. 'Would it be a bad thing if I was?'

'Yes,' she said. Something told her he wouldn't be an easy man to walk away from. Not disposable, like the others. 'Stop it. I have no desire to become a notch on what I understand is your very crowded bedpost.'

Luca regarded her for a moment. In her top and jeans, arms crossed, a frown knitting her brows, she looked quite fierce. But Luca knew women. He knew them well.

And Mia McKenzie was definitely protesting too much.

His gaze slipped to her mouth. 'Are you sure?'

Mia felt her lips tingle beneath his heated stare and felt her resistance ebb. *Now, he was something that could make her forget for a little while.*

Luca grinned, pleased to have discomforted her. 'Goodnight, Mia. Don't let the bed bugs bite.'

By four a.m. Luca was ready to head home. The craziness had settled and things were quiet—for now anyway.

He'd checked on the MVA from earlier—the laparotomy had found a perforated bowel. Stan had been admitted to the psych unit on a ninety-six-hour hold. The baby was settled into the special care nursery for overnight monitoring.

And his paperwork was up to date.

Just one last thing to do—check on Mia.

He hesitated, his hand on the doorknob of the on-call room. Prickly little Mia probably wouldn't appreciate being checked up on.

Her prim *I have no desire to become a notch on what I understand is your very crowded bedpost,* had played on his mind ever since she'd uttered it.

She obviously disapproved.

What the hell was wrong with indulging in a little flirtation here and there? Spending an enjoyable few hours with a woman who was fully aware that one night was all he was interested in?

He was always open and honest about his intentions. And he never made the mistake of giving false hope by going back for seconds. He knew his limitations where relationships were concerned—had learned them at a very early age.

Best not to set expectations—that way you couldn't let anyone down.

He loved women—bronzed, natural, fun-loving Australian women in particular—and they loved him. And he was a healthy adult male.

Still, Mia intrigued him. Her resistance even more so. He'd be lying if he said he didn't want her.

He twisted the knob and opened the door. She wasn't around and the light had been turned out. Sleeping room one had its door shut and he padded over to it, knocking lightly when he reached his destination.

No reply was forthcoming. He hesitated again before gently twisting the knob and opening the door a crack—checking on her *was* the right thing to do.

The sight stopped him in his tracks.

She had fallen asleep in a semi-upright foetal position on the triple-seater couch. Her head was snuggled against the fat cushions of the sofa, her spine propped up against the squishy arm, her legs, tucked in close to her bottom, had fallen sideways to rest against the back of the couch.

She'd taken her hair out of its clasp and it fanned around her shoulders and the couch cushions. Her feet were bare. A medical journal lay open on her chest.

The lamp on the table beside the couch illuminated her relaxed profile in a warm yellow glow. His gaze tracked the outline of her nose, the slope of one cheekbone, the plump fullness of her mouth.

He was satisfied to see the journal on her chest rise and fell in a regular rhythm. His eyes dropped to the white dressing covering her upper arm and he absently noted there was no fresh ooze.

She was obviously fine.

As he watched, a little frown wrinkled her forehead and a soft mew escaped her mouth. He wondered what she was dreaming about. Her near-death experience? The flash of a blade? The bawling of a baby?

His question—*are you sure?*—from earlier?

She mewed again and he realised he was staring at a sleeping woman who would most definitely not appreciate the attention. He left the door ajar and turned away.

Mia was trapped in a dream she didn't seem able to fight her way out of. It was one she hadn't had since she'd been a little girl but it was disjointed, jumping back and forth between now and then. Between Stan and her father. Each slash of the knife through the air shunting the dream to the other person, to another time.

Her mother was there too somewhere, holding a

wrapped bundle that Mia knew was her stillborn sister. Her mother was sobbing those deep, gut-wrenching sobs that had been indelibly woven through the fabric of Mia's life.

She was holding her father's hand, her little ten-year-old fingers tugging at his long ones, asking him not to go. And then Stan would yell to get back, get back as the knifepoint came ever closer.

Daddy, don't go. Don't go.
Slash. Back, get back. Slash.
Please, Daddy, don't go.
Slash. Slash. Back! Get back!
Daddy!

'Daddy, come back!'

Luca was almost at the door when he heard her cry out. Without thinking, he hurried back to her, pushed open the door and strode over to the couch as Mia cried out again, flinging her head from side to side. The journal had already fallen to the floor.

Luca took her by the shoulders and gave her a gentle shake, mindful of her injury. 'Mia! Mia.'

Mia heard a voice. A different voice. And the urge to run towards it, to run away from the feelings of hopelessness, was overwhelming.

Luca? Luca?

'Mia.' He shook her again. 'It's Luca. Wake up. Wake up.'

Mia's eyes flew open. *Luca?* Luca was here?

The mellow lamplight bathed his strong masculine features, softening them—his jaw, his cheeks, his mouth—and he finally looked like that angel. She blinked away the crazy thought as tendrils of dread clung to every heartbeat.

Mia tried to sit up but her limbs wouldn't co-operate and her arm throbbed. 'Luca?'

'Shh,' he murmured, the pads of his thumbs absently stroking her shoulders. Her large blue eyes reflected her confusion. 'It's okay, you were having a bad dream.'

Mia nodded. 'It was…there was…'

'Your father?'

Mia blinked up at him. He pronounced the *th* softly, giving the word a gentleness it hadn't had in the dream. Her head was crowded with memories. One after the other, battering her brains and beating against the locked door to her heart.

Old and long forgotten. Supposedly.

She had to make them stop.

'Are you okay?' Luca asked.

She looked at him, into eyes so deep and brown it was like falling into a well.

He could make them stop.

'Mia?'

She shook her head. 'Not yet.' *But she would be.*

Then she leaned forward and pressed her lips to his.

Luca stilled at the tentative touch. He pulled back and searched her eyes. 'Mia?'

She shook her head and, supporting herself on her good arm, leant in close, locking her gaze with his. 'Kiss me,' she murmured, her mouth a whisper from his.

In fact, she was close enough that Luca could almost feel those two little words branding his lips from the sudden heat rising between their bodies. He dropped his gaze to her mouth—so near, so luscious—and he was instantly hard.

'What happened to not wanting to be a notch on my bedpost?'

'Stan,' she muttered.

After that Luca wasn't sure who closed the hair's-breadth between them. But he did seize control.

His mouth opened over hers and demanded she follow suit. And follow him she did, opening to him eagerly. He thrust his tongue into her mouth and the little whimper at the back of her throat implored him to keep going.

He tunnelled his hands into her hair, angling her head back to accommodate more, and the kiss escalated. Got deeper, wetter, hotter. His body moved over hers, forcing her knees down, crowding her back against the cushions, imprisoning her against the couch, her head falling back over the arm.

His hand brushed the side of her breast and she moaned deep and low. He drew it lower, to her waist, her hip as his mouth broke from hers to ravage her neck, stretched out before him, the pulse at the base beating as madly as his own.

Mia felt the memories disappear into the ether as a veritable storm of sensations swept through her body.

Yes, yes, yes.

'Yes,' she cried out as Luca licked along her collar bone. 'Yes,' as he nipped at the base of her neck. 'Yes,' as his hand squeezed the exact spot where, beneath her jeans, butt met thigh.

One-handed, she pulled his polo shirt out of his jeans and ruched it up his back, his skin hot and vibrant beneath her palm. She kept pulling till it was past his shoulders and gave a triumphant cry when Luca ducked his head through the opening and she pulled it off him entirely.

His smooth chest was totally bare to her touch and she pressed a kiss to a flat brown pec, then his collarbone, then the hollow at the base of his neck.

She breathed him in, his scent intoxicating. Potent. Virile. Male. It filled up her senses. Like a drug.

And left her wanting more.

He claimed her mouth again, pressing her deep into the cushions, and she revelled in his weight, in the tangle of his legs, in the oh-so-right angle of his pelvis.

Luca felt the agitated circling of her hips and ground himself against her. He swallowed her gasp, making her moan more deeply as his hand travelled back up her body, pushing beneath her top. He needed to touch her breasts. To see them. Taste them. To feel them rubbing against his chest.

He pushed the fabric up, his hand filling with soft, delectable female. Satin, lace and heaven all in one sweet handful. He rubbed the hard point with his thumb and she gasped.

Luca broke away from her mouth, his lips instinctively following the dictates of his body as his tongue stroked down her neck, over her collarbone, the slope of her breast then finally her nipple. The lace was rough against his tongue as he sucked the tip right through the material of the bra.

Mia's breath hissed out as her back arched involuntarily. It jarred painfully through her sore arm and she cried out in pain this time, her eyes squeezing shut.

'Mia?' Luca broke away. 'Oh, sorry, did I hurt your arm?'

Mia shook her head, her eyes still shut. 'It's okay, it's settling.'

Luca groaned, dropping his forehead onto her chest. Her heart beat frantically there as her ribcage heaved in and out. His own breathing was loud and ragged in the silence.

Mia's eyes slowly fluttered open as the pain ebbed. She looked down at his head, his thick wavy hair tousled from their ministrations. It was suddenly absurdly funny and she felt a bubble of laughter rise in her chest. She bit down on her lip to stop it from spilling out.

But her ribcage shook with the effort to keep it in and it bubbled up anyway.

Luca felt the vibration against his forehead and glanced up just as she laughed. Their breathing was still erratic, they were both half-undressed and thoroughly bedraggled, he had a raging hard-on—and she was laughing.

It was absurd. So he laughed too.

'You're crazy,' he said after their laughter had died down.

Mia shook her head. 'This is crazy.'

Luca had to agree. Even if his hard-on didn't. 'You want to stop?' he murmured.

His husky voice thickened his accent and a surge of lust welled deep down low in her. Mia shook her head. She couldn't have stopped now even if a bus had crashed right through the walls of the on-call room.

She was a healthy adult woman, and it had been a couple of weeks since her last liaison. 'That would be even crazier.'

Luca grinned, dropping his mouth to her chest, run-

ning his nose lightly along the slope of a breast and upwards to nuzzle her neck. 'Pure insanity.'

She stretched her neck to give him better access.
'Certifiable,' she agreed.

Luca laved the pulse half way up her neck with his
tongue. 'Utter lunacy.'

'I think we should get the door, though,' she managed through the haze of lust descending on her.

Luca's head snapped to the doorway. He swore softly
against her neck at its partially open state and was re-
warded with another throaty laugh. He kissed her hard
on the mouth.

'Take your clothes off,' he said, before pushing off
her, padding over to the door and locking it.

'You do realise this is a one-off, right?' she said as
she tried to wiggle out of her jeans essentially one-
handed.

Luca turned and watched her. He could clearly see
her nipples through the lace of her bra and it made him
harder.

He undid his zip and peeled off his jeans. 'Of course.
My bedpost is littered with one-offs. Or hadn't you
heard?'

Mia went to grin but it died on her lips as the pure
male beauty of his physique was fully exposed to her.
Long, lean legs, dusted with black hair. Flat, flat belly.
Broad in the shoulder, narrow in the hip.

And if the bulge in his snug cotton boxers was anything to go by, large, in all the right places.

She'd seen a marble statue just like him in Rome
many years before. Luca di Angelo had *Made in Italy*
stamped all over him.

Then he came to her, towering over her, snapping the

lamp off, helping her out of her jeans, kissing her everywhere, arching her back over the arm of the lounge, thrusting her breasts upwards towards his eager mouth. Making her sigh. Making her whimper. Making her come.

And, best of all, making her forget.

Three days later Dr Finn Kennedy, chief of Surgery, strode into the emergency department on what he was sure was going to be a fool's errand. He was tired. His upper arm had ached all night despite several shots of whisky, and he rubbed at it absently. His eyes felt scratchy and his damn nuisance thumb was numb and tingly.

He pulled up short as Evie approached him. Great, just what he needed. Dr Evie Lockheart. *Princess Evie.* Born with a silver spoon in her mouth, working in her granddaddy's hospital, a place still generously supported by the Lockheart family trust and her father in particular, who was treated like royalty by the boffins upstairs.

With absolutely no idea how hard ordinary people had it.

And the only woman in the entire hospital who seemed to be able to push his buttons. She didn't simper or cower. Just looked at him patiently with those damn hazel eyes.

'Dr Kennedy,' she greeted him.

'There's a consult for me?' he asked, not bothering to acknowledge her greeting. He had a feeling that she saw beyond his curt exterior and he didn't like it.

The only other woman to have done that had been

Lydia—his brother's widow—and that had been an un-mitigated disaster.

Evie refused to give Finn the satisfaction of seeing how his brusqueness grated. He wasn't in the army any more and she wasn't one of his soldiers to be ordered around. Instead, she launched straight into her spiel. Still, it didn't stop her heart from pounding like a run-away train in her chest—she'd made an amazing inci-dental find and despite his gruffness she was desperate for his approval.

'Twenty-two-year-old female, with a painful lump in her breast. Ultrasound identified a small benign cyst—'

'Are you kidding me?' Finn glared down at her, hands on hips. 'You do know I'm a cardiac surgeon, right? That means stuff to do with the heart.'

Evie held his gaze and her tongue and continued as if he hadn't just rudely interrupted her. 'She also com-plained of fatigue, shortness of breath and intermittent chest pains. Incidental finding reveals bicuspid aortic valve with associated ascending aortic aneurysm.'

Finn stared at her. Was in hell was she on about? 'Sure,' he said sarcastically as he held out his hand. 'Radiographer report?'

'There isn't one. Radiology was backlogged and the ultrasound was performed in the department.'

'I see. By who, exactly?' he demanded.

Evie's gaze didn't waver as his piercing blue eyes dared her to blink. 'By me.'

Finn snorted. 'You? You diagnosed a complex heart condition through a breast ultrasound?'

Evie crossed her arms too. 'Yes.'

'That's not even remotely possible,' he snapped.

Until right now, Evie would have agreed. 'It is if the woman in question has very small breasts.'

Finn glared at her. Princess Evie—her place at the prestigious SHH emergency department no doubt paid for by her father's huge donations—wasting his time. 'Where's the patient?'

'Cubicle fifteen,' she said calmly.

'What have you told her that I'm going to have to untell her?' he asked silkily.

'I told her I couldn't get a good enough angle and I was going to call for someone more experienced,' Evie bristled. 'I did *go* to medical school, Dr Kennedy,' she said frostily.

'Really? Daddy couldn't fast-track you, then?'

Evie ignored the dig. 'I graduated top of my year.'

'He gives to the university too, then?' Finn retorted, before turning on his heel and heading for the indicated cubicle.

Evie's heart tripped in her chest as she struggled to keep up with his long-legged stride. But even falling flat on her face would be worth it just to see the look on Finn's when her diagnosis was confirmed.

Finn snapped back the curtain and introduced himself to a petite young woman in a hospital gown who was chewing on her bottom lip. He smiled at her. 'Hello. Bethany, is it?' he asked, consulting her chart. 'I'm Dr Kennedy. Dr Lockheart's asked me to have a look at you.'

'Is something wrong?' Bethany asked, looking from one doctor to the other.

Finn patted her hand. 'Give me one minute and I'll be able to tell you.'

He turned away to the compact mobile ultrasound

machine and shot Evie an exasperated look. It was hardly the most sophisticated machine in their radiology arsenal. He found it hard to believe anyone could diagnose a potentially fatal heart problem on something so basic.

He picked up the transducer from its cradle fiddled with the pulse settings and the screen brightness and turned to back to Bethany, who'd already opened her gown and put her arm above her head.

Finn squeezed a blob of warmed gel on Bethany's chest, noting that she did indeed have practically non-existent breast tissue. 'Okay, here goes,' he murmured as he ploughed the transducer through the middle of the gel.

He ignored Evie, who was standing at his elbow, and concentrated on the small screen as the grainy grey and black image of Bethany's pumping heart came into view. It took him less than a minute to concur with Evie's very impressive diagnosis.

He flicked a glance at her and met her unwavering hazel gaze. There was no triumph or smugness there, just complete confidence in her diagnosis, and he felt a rather foreign feeling of grudging respect.

Maybe there was more to her than the Lockheart name.

'Is everything okay?' Bethany asked.

Finn shook his head. 'No. There's a problem,' he admitted. 'But it's okay,' he added quickly. 'I can fix it.'

Evie listened in awe while Finn sat with Bethany and explained how the small benign-looking cyst in her breast was nothing compared to the real problem, and what he could do about it. For such an arrogant, rude, human being he had amazing rapport with patients.

When they walked out of the curtain thirty minutes later Evie had seen an entirely different side to the infamous Dr Finn Kennedy. She'd known he must have had a heart in there somewhere but it was the first time she'd ever seen any evidence of it.

'Organise a bed for her in CCU,' Finn said briskly, handing Bethany's chart to her.

Evie nodded as she accepted it, trying not to feel discouraged. She hadn't really thought he'd congratulate her, had she?

'Good catch, Dr Lockheart,' he murmured. 'Maybe you're not Daddy's little girl after all.'

And then he turned in the opposite direction and strode away.

Evie blinked as the back-handed compliment sank in.

High praise indeed!

CHAPTER THREE

WHEN Mia came on duty later that afternoon the first person she spied was Luca. Which wasn't difficult, given that his very presence seemed to attract attention. She'd bet whoever had invented the term *chick magnet* had met Luca di Angelo.

Of course, she could also just have conjured him up—she couldn't deny she'd been thinking about him and their illicit liaison in the on-call room a little too often on her days off.

She squeezed her eyes shut tight for a few seconds then opened them again. Nope—still there.

And looking right at her.

Smiling at her, actually. Like he knew all her dirty secrets. And that he was one of them.

She graced him with an indifferent glare and a cool nod of the head as she slung her stethoscope around her neck and deliberately walked in the opposite direction.

Luca chuckled to himself as he watched the hypnotic swish of her blonde ponytail. She seemed all prim and neat, her dark grey tailored trousers classically elegant, her high-necked, capped-sleeve blouse in sapphire blue crisp and stylish.

Not a wrinkle. Or a hair out of place.

Very different from the Mia of the other night. Who had looked rumpled and disturbed and hadn't cared about either.

A hum coursed through his blood at the mere thought. It certainly hadn't been the way he had envisaged that night would turn out. In fact, if someone had asked him who'd be the woman least likely to sleep with him, he would have said Mia McKenzie.

But it had been pretty damn amazing. Once she'd made up her mind she hadn't held back. She hadn't done that irritating talking/fishing-for-compliments thing that a surprising amount of women did during sex. Or tried to twist herself into some uncomfortable position because she knew it was her best angle.

She hadn't even asked him what he liked in an effort to make it all about him.

No. She'd known exactly what she'd wanted and she'd taken it. But she'd given, too. She'd been confident and assured and had met him as an equal.

It was the most uncomplicated one-off he'd ever had.

Now, if he could just stop thinking about it…

Mia moved through the shift with her senses on high alert. Her skin prickled when he was near. The hairs on her nape stood to attention. Her nipples seemed to stay in a state of permanent erection. It seemed every cell in her body was well and truly tuned in to Luca.

And it didn't help that they kept running into each other.

The first time had been in the lift after she'd been on for half an hour. She'd just caught it before the doors had shut and squeezed in with several other people sharing the space with a transport bed. The patient had been almost lost amidst the equipment on the bed and the stuff hanging off the rails had made it an even tighter fit.

She'd smiled at the patient as the doors had shut and turned to stare at the opposite wall, only to be confronted by Luca's slow, sexy smile.

'Dr McKenzie,' he murmured.

'Dr di Angelo,' she replied, dropping her gaze to the knot of his tie rather than the knowing look in his eyes.

'How were your days off?' he asked innocently.

Mia couldn't believe how intimate it could feel between them in a lift full of onlookers. She kept her gaze firmly on the knot at his throat.

His long, tanned throat she'd licked every inch of.

'Fine, thank you.' *Apart from daydreaming about you.*

His grin broadened as if he could hear the words she hadn't said. 'I trust your arm is getting better?'

Mia had felt sure that if his voice could cure wounds hers would have miraculously healed on the spot. She kept her gaze resolute, trying not to think how erotic the smooth glide of his jaw had been against her breasts.

'Thank you, yes.'

'I can look at it later, if you like. I think there're still some dressings left in the on-call room.'

Mia's eyes flicked up before she could stop them and his smile gained a slight triumphant edge. A blast of heat arced between them and Mia was surprised that it hadn't incinerated everyone in the lift.

'Thank you Dr di Angelo. I can manage,' she murmured as the lift doors opened and she walked out on legs that felt like wobbly jelly.

The second time she'd worked with him on a fifty-two-year-old construction worker who had come in from an industrial accident, having sustained major chest and abdominal injuries. He'd placed a chest tube and done the intubation while she'd inserted a central line.

They'd worked in tandem, like a well-oiled machine, but she'd been aware of him and his every move every second. Their gazes had locked regularly. At one stage their heads had even bumped together, competing for the same line of sight. He'd apologised, but their faces had been very close. His gaze had dropped briefly to her mouth and her mind had strayed to exactly where she'd put it on his body.

The third time she'd been plastering a fifteen-year-old-boy's broken arm when he'd lounged in the doorway to the plaster room. He hadn't announced himself but something had alerted her and she'd looked up to find him propped against the doorframe.

'Haven't you got something better to be doing?' she asked testily, returning her attention to the job. How was she supposed to avoid him when he seemed to be wherever she was?

Luca shook his head. 'All quiet. I thought I'd *skulk* here for a while.'

She'd glanced up at his use of the word 'skulk' and he grinned at her. He advanced into the room and she tried not to notice how his beautifully cut trousers and khaki business shirt fitted him to perfection. He could easily have been strutting a Milan catwalk.

'You the boy who was having a light-sabre fight with your little sister?' he asked the teenager.

The boy nodded glumly. 'She's never going to let me live it down.'

'Sisters can be very unforgiving.'

'You've got sisters?'

Luca nodded. 'Three.'

'Man, that's harsh.'

Mia slid him a sly glance. His accent had thickened and his words had seemed tinged with something she hadn't been able to put her finger on. Then the two of them got into a conversation about *Star Wars* and Mia gritted her teeth and pretended Luca and his mouth were in a galaxy far, far away.

By the time he passed her in the hallway at ten o'clock she was walking a very fine line between homicidal mania and sexual frustration. The man was everywhere—in the department and in her head—and, heaven help her, she wanted to push him into the nearest available private space and tear his clothes off.

But it had been a one-off.

They'd agreed.

'Oh, Dr McKenzie, I meant to tell you earlier, I've arranged for a debrief session with John Allen from Psych for you.'

Mia slowed and turned. How could she want to kill him and kiss at the same time? 'Cos she did. *She wanted to kiss that smug Sicilian mouth so badly she could scream.*

'I don't need a damn debrief,' she snapped, tossing her head, daring him to push her. 'I'm fine.'

Luca smiled at the flash in her eyes—like sun shining on a cathedral window. He liked the way her chest rose and fell just a little bit too fast. And how it pulled at her blouse in all the right places.

He pushed back. 'I'm sure you are. But you're having one, anyway.'

That was it! Mia put her hands on her hips, barely

suppressing the juvenile urge to stamp her foot. 'Oh, no, I'm not.'

He nodded. 'Ten tomorrow morning.'

Her gaze locked on his mouth the same time his locked on hers. Something stirred deep in her belly. A primal recognition of attraction. A potent force.

She lifted her chin. 'You can't make me.'

Luca felt a subtle shift in the signals emanating from her. Had that challenge been sexual? A nurse bustled past and gave them a strange look.

Luca inclined his head to a nearby door. 'Shall we discuss this in private?'

Mia knew it was the on-call room. 'Fine,' she muttered, her heart rate suddenly trebling.

She followed him through the open doorway into the empty room. 'I'm not seeing a shrink, Luca. You can—'

Luca turned abruptly, cutting her off with a swift, hard kiss, crowding her back towards the door, shutting it with the combined weight of their two bodies.

Every cell in Mia's body leapt to life. She grabbed the knot of his tie, pulling him flush against her.

She groaned, or was it him?

Madness, it was madness.

She broke off. 'We said once,' she gasped.

Luca nodded. 'I know.' And then he went back for more.

Mia gave herself up to the urgent press of his mouth. The bold stroke of his hand against her breast. The hard thrust of his erection.

She whimpered as he ground his pelvis into hers and rubbed herself shamelessly against him. Her hands travelled to his butt, urging him closer, nearer, angling him just right.

She shut her eyes as he hit the spot, her head lolling back against the door. His mouth moved lower to the mad flutter at the side of her neck.

The flutter was everywhere. In her breasts and her belly and between her legs. It thrummed through her ears in a deafening thunder like the roar of the ocean or the call of the wild.

Luca. Luca. Luca.

Not even the peeling of an emergency beeper pierced it. It took two squealing beepers to manage that.

Mia pushed on Luca's chest as the sound finally penetrated. They were both gasping, their clothes askew as they automatically reached for their pagers.

Damn! 'Cardiac arrest two minutes out,' Mia panted.

Luca nodded as he read the same message on his beeper. 'Great timing,' he murmured.

Mia took a few seconds to straighten her clothes and clear the heavy fog of lust from her brain. Luca followed suit.

'How do I look?' she asked as she quickly retied her hair to its pristine smoothness.

Luca smiled. 'Like you've been thoroughly kissed.'

Mia glared at him.

That was exactly what she'd been afraid of!

The following night, Mia snuggled into her ancient duffle coat as she and Evie left The Harbour behind them and crossed over the road, heading for the flashing neon sign that read 'Pete's'. It was nearly ten o'clock but Wednesday was traditionally staff discount night— if you could produce an SHH badge, drinks were half-price—it was an ingrained part of The Harbour's culture.

Not that the majority of people letting their hair down at tables needed to produce ID. Pete, the owner, had been running the popular bar for the last twenty years and not only knew who was who but usually who was doing who as well.

Of course he would never have disclosed such information. Like every good barkeeper, discretion was his middle name. And it was definitely the reason why Pete's had been *the* hangout for SHH staff over the years.

Sure, proximity and comfy booths also helped but when down-time was limited, a cosy place nearby where a busy professional could talk and unwind and not be *on* for a while or worry about gossip, which was already rife enough in their work environment, was definitely appreciated.

He was also fiercely protective of the hard-working staff at Sydney's most prestigious hospital. He didn't tolerate customers who complained to him about bias or hassled his favourite clients in any way. After all, the good staff of The Harbour had been his bread and butter since he'd opened.

But it was more than that. The doctors and nurses of the SHH were special. Too many times he'd seen them walk through his door with weary, haunted expressions. They saw things on a day-to-day basis that were the stuff of most people's nightmares. And if a drink or two at his bar managed to take their minds off that then Pete considered he'd done a good day's work.

Mia welcomed the blast of heat as Evie opened the heavy wooden door to Pete's. They shrugged out of their coats and headed to the bar, greeting several people they knew along the way.

'It's freezing out there,' she said to Pete, thrusting out her hands. 'Just feel these.'

Pete smiled at them and dutifully folded Mia's chilly fingers in his big warm mitts. 'Cold hands, warm heart,' he quipped.

Mia grinned at him. 'You are a romantic.'

'Nothing wrong with that, love. Right, Evie?'

Evie, distracted by Finn chatting to a busty blonde further along the bar, answered automatically. 'Right.'

'Pete, Pete, Pete,' Mia tutted. 'Romance belongs in books.'

'Maybe you should read a couple,' he jested.

'Books? We don't have time for books, do we, Evie?' Mia asked.

'Nope,' Evie murmured, sliding a surreptitious gaze towards Finn.

'Journals are all I get a chance to read,' Mia lamented.

Pete sighed. 'No time for a man either, I suppose?'

'There are men,' she protested. Being happily married for thirty years had rendered Pete's vision permanently rose coloured.

Pete gave her a reproachful look. 'Men, sure. But one man, Mia? That's what you need.'

Mia rolled her eyes. 'If I were a man, would we be having this conversation?' She looked around and spied Finn with a vaguely familiar blonde—Suzy someone? One of the scrub nurses from the OT. 'Do you say this sort of stuff to Finn?'

Pete clutched his heart in a wounded fashion. He was

like the SHH fairy godfather, wanting happily-ever-afters for *all* his regulars.

'Of course. I say it to Finn most of all.' He deliberately looked at a distracted Evie. 'That man needs the love of a good woman more than anyone.'

Evie looked at Pete sharply and didn't say anything for a beat or two. 'I'll have a tequila shot followed by a bottle of lager, thank you, Peter.'

'Just the usual for me,' Mia added.

He grinned at them. 'Okay, okay. I can take a hint.'

Pete served Evie's shot first and she snatched it up and threw it straight down her throat, revelling in the burn. As she slammed it back on the bar she glanced Finn's way. He was looking at her with those piercing blue eyes and for a moment their gazes locked.

Was that disdain? Judgement? Disapproval?

Too bad, so sad.

'Orange juice for you,' Pete said, placing it on the bar in front of Mia. 'Beer for Evie.'

Evie picked up her drink. 'Let's go over there,' she said, moving off the bar stool in the opposite direction to Finn, before Mia even had a chance to lift her juice. She shrugged at Pete and followed.

Unfortunately, Evie was heading to a booth Mia would rather not be at but it was difficult to change direction now the occupants had spotted them and waved them over. And she didn't want to have to explain to her friend who would no doubt put two and two together and come up with five.

'Move over,' Evie announced. 'We're coming in.'

Mia tried not to look at Luca as she was forced to take the seat next to him. But she could feel his eyes on hers and the heat of him immediately enveloped her as her body responded in an almost Pavlovian fashion to his proximity.

The booth was spacious but with three bodies either side it was a cosy fit.

'Mia, long time no see.'

Mia smiled at John Allen, the psychologist she'd been forced to see that morning by Luca. Susie, his wife, was also there and greeted Mia warmly. Of course she saw them regularly enough anyway, given that they too lived at the nearby Kirribilli Views apartments where a lot of The Harbour staff resided.

'How did the debrief go?' Luca enquired.

'Mia's fine.' John winked.

She glared at him. 'I *am* fine.'

'Sure,' he soothed.

'You know, Mia, it's not a bad thing, to talk this kind of thing through.' Rupert Davidson, head of Neurology, entered the conversation.

'He's right,' Teo Tuala, SHH's head of Paediatrics, agreed.

Mia looked at all of them, exasperation bubbling inside her. She inclined her head towards Luca. 'He didn't. He was being threatened too.'

'Yes, but I wasn't lunged at with a knife. Neither did I have my arm slashed open by said knife.'

Mia took a long swig of her drink as his voice, so close to her ear, took her right back to the on-call room. 'I'm fine,' she repeated.

'Well, you know where I am if you want to talk any more,' John offered.

Mia couldn't help but think that a sweaty twenty minutes with Luca had helped more than an hour's conversation with John but it was a dangerous path for her thoughts to take given how aware she was of Luca right now.

'Absolutely.' She nodded. 'What's happening with Stan?' she asked, deftly moving the focus of the conversation off her. 'His ninety-six-hour hold must be up by now.'

John nodded. 'He's staying on voluntarily. He's had increasing paranoia episodes over the last few years apparently. We want to get his meds right and get him well supported before we discharge him.'

Mia nodded and soon the conversation drifted to other subjects.

Ten minutes later, Evie finished her beer and stood. 'Gotta go. I promised my father I'd drop by some hideous dinner party he's having. He's sending a car for me.'

Mia leapt at the opportunity to escape and stood as well. 'I'd better go too. I'm on in the morning.'

'Oh, Mia, no,' Susie objected. 'Don't leave me alone with all these men talking shop. Stay a bit longer.'

Mia looked at Susie's beseeching gaze and acquiesced. It had absolutely nothing to do with every cell suddenly crying out for Luca's heat to be squashed back up against her again. 'Okay, I guess I can stay for one more.'

'I'll get another round,' Luca said. He climbed out of the booth and watched bemused as Mia took a step back. 'Is that vodka and orange?'

Mia shook her head. 'Just orange.'

He frowned. 'You're not on call, are you?'

'Nope. Just not drinking.'

Luca slid a glance at the table, where the merits of a journal article were being debated. He looked back at

Mia. 'Are you worried you may lose your inhibitions?' he murmured, dropping his voice a little. 'I don't need alcohol to lose mine.'

Mia, aware of how close he was standing, felt the pronunciation of *inhibitions* slide right down her spine. His English was perfect but the occasional word leant towards his native Italian.

'I wasn't aware you had any,' she said, her voice steely.

Luca walked away chuckling, deep and low. Unfortunately, that was exactly where Mia felt it—deep and low.

Standing at the bar a couple of minutes later, Luca rattled off the drinks order and waited for Pete to return with them.

'Here you are, Luca,' Pete said, placing them on a round tray.

'Thanks.' Luca handed over the money.

'You're with Mia, I see,' Pete said casually. 'Great girl.'

Luca nodded, his gaze straying back to a smiling Mia. She was wearing a long skirt, a turtle-neck skivvy and black knee-high boots. He'd been fantasising about her in those boots, just the boots, all day.

'Yes,' he agreed. Except they weren't the words he'd have used. Sexy, feisty, prickly seemed to suit her so much better.

'Fantastic doctor,' Pete pressed, joining Luca in his observation of Mia.

Now, those were words Luca would use. 'Yes, she is,' he agreed.

'Hard to believe someone like that's still single,' Pete mused.

Luca looked back at the bartender. 'And why is that, do you think?'

Pete looked Luca direct in the eye. 'Men these days scare too easily. They buy into her *I'm fine* exterior.'

'And she's not?'

Pete shook his head. 'Of course she's not. She just doesn't know it yet.'

They watched her again for a moment or two. 'But don't tell her I told you that,' Pete added.

Luca laughed, picking up the tray. 'Deal.'

'So, Luca.' Susie, desperate for a topic change, watched Luca slip back in beside Mia. 'Sicily, huh?'

Luca nodded as the familiar feeling of dread and loss and yearning threatened to swamp him. He pushed them back. 'That's right.'

Mia glanced at Luca as she felt his thigh, jammed against hers, tense. This close to his delectable profile she could see the clench of his jaw.

'Where exactly?' Susie continued, unaware of Luca's reluctance to talk about his past. Especially his home.

Luca forced himself to breathe out, to loosen the suddenly tense muscles of his neck. 'Marsala.'

'Like the wine?' she asked.

Luca nodded. 'Yes. Like the wine.'

'We never got to Sicily,' Susie said. 'But we adored Italy, didn't we, John?'

John nodded. 'Europe as a whole. We're actually going skiing in France at the end of the year.'

Luca slowly relaxed each muscle group as conversation moved to travel but a pall had been cast over the evening. If it wasn't for the alluring press of Mia against his side, he'd have excused himself almost immediately.

But her nearness held him in check. He'd been aware of her since she'd first entered the bar and he could tell she was more than aware of him. There was a crackle between them that had nothing to do with the delicious rub of their thighs.

And after the way the conversation had turned tonight he couldn't think of a better way of keeping the memories of Marsala at bay than getting lost in Mia for a while.

To hell with their one-off pact.

Teo drained his cola and stood. 'I have to go back to The Harbour and check on a patient then I'd better head home. Emma's teething and keeping Zoe and me up most of the night.'

'Teething already?' Susie marvelled. 'Isn't six months a little early?'

Teo shook his head. 'Every baby is different.' And he grinned at them because even with the sleepless nights, Zoe and Emma had made him happier than he'd ever thought possible.

'Aw,' Rupert, also happily married, teased. 'Ain't love grand?'

Mia, barely able to suppress an eye roll at Teo's goofy expression, saw her second chance at escape. 'Yep, me too. Early start.'

'Same here,' Luca said, letting her out. 'I'll walk you to your car.'

Mia felt a thickening in the air between them as their gazes skittered past each other. Yep, like that's what she needed right now. *Sex-on-legs escorting her anywhere.*

But, sensing he was as desperate to get away as she was, she nodded her head graciously. They said their goodbyes and made their way through the throng to the coat stands by the front door.

'I'm not driving,' Mia said as she shrugged into her coat. 'I live just down at Kirribilli Views. I walk to work. I don't need an escort.'

Luca smiled as he adjusted the collar on his suit jacket. 'What a coincidence. So do I.'

Mia's fingers fumbled with the tie of her coat. *Of course he did.* 'Of course you do,' she said faintly. She hadn't seen him around but it was a big place populated with shift workers.

Luca chuckled as he opened the heavy wooden door and gestured for her to precede him. He looked back over his shoulder as he departed. Pete grinned and gave him a thumbs-up.

CHAPTER FOUR

MIA buried her hands in her coat pockets as her warm breath fogged into the night air. She glanced at Luca, who had only his suit jacket to fend off cold winter fingers. But he looked warm and vital—like a walking hot-water bottle. She shook the tempting image of her wrapped around him in bed from her head. It was disconcerting to say the least when the streets were dark and practically deserted and they kept passing interesting alcoves and alleyways where two people could warm up really quickly.

Mia clamped down on the direction of her thoughts and the strange undulation of her pelvic floor muscles. 'Aren't you cold in that?' she groused.

Luca shrugged. 'Two beers help.'

Mia nodded. 'I don't drink much,' she replied.

Why she felt the need to share that she had no idea, but she could feel his pull and knew she was on a slow march towards an inevitable ending. This wasn't how it was supposed to be between them and she felt suddenly nervous.

'You don't like it?' Luca enquired.

Mia shook her head. 'I went through a stage where I liked it a little too much.'

'Ah,' Luca said, intrigued by the nugget of information. Was this what Pete had alluded to? 'Care to elaborate?'

Not bloody likely! Mia couldn't believe she'd told him that much. Damn this man! But there was something about him, a recognition that they were the same, that seemed to loosen her lips around him. Still, she had absolutely no intention of reliving two years of booze and bad men with him.

The past was the past.

'No,' she said. He quirked an eyebrow at her and she said, 'It's complicated.'

They walked in silence for a few moments. 'I suppose a man from Marsala probably doesn't understand that.'

Luca tensed. He'd been enjoying the build-up between them as each footstep took them closer to their apartments. To their beds. The footpath had narrowed and their arms brushed; her body warmth mixed and flirted with his. Their footsteps matched, their breathing synchronised.

But suddenly that was forgotten.

Mia turned her head to face him. 'How long ago did you leave?'

Luca bit down on the urge to laugh at her choice of words. Leaving implied consent. He hadn't been given a whole lot of choice. 'I was sixteen.'

She whistled. 'That's a long time.'

Luca chuckled, trying to divert the conversation. 'Are you implying I'm old?'

Mia laughed too and let it peter out. 'You're a long way from home, Luca,' she mused.

Although she, more than anyone, knew that geographic proximity had nothing to do with that sense of 'home'. She'd grown up a twenty-minute drive from here and it may as well have been Italy for all the connection Mia felt to the brick and mortar house where her mother still resided. Mainly on the couch.

Luca kept his gaze firmly fixed on the illuminated arch of the Sydney Harbour Bridge he could just see through the treetops. 'Yes.'

Mia smiled. 'Care to elaborate?'

'No.'

'Word on the grapevine is you studied medicine in London. I thought Italian mamas liked to keep tabs on their sons. No decent universities in Italy?'

Luca saw his mother's broken face again on that horrible day that had changed everything. The sorrow and disappointment etched in lines that had seemed somehow instantly deeper. He schooled his expression as he looked at Mia and repeated her response.

'It's complicated.'

Mia nodded. If anyone understood that, she did. And she understood the underlying message—butt out. She got that too.

They lapsed into silence again but she was aware of him large and silent beside her. Aware of his tension and his potent, brooding masculinity.

'Here we are,' she announced unnecessarily as the doors to the ten-storey apartment complex loomed ahead.

Luca dragged himself out of the sticky web of his past. 'Yes,' he murmured. He looked down at her. 'Your place or mine?'

Mia swallowed. She should have been outraged at his assumption. But he was looking at her intently with that devil mouth and heat was flooding through her belly and tightening her breasts.

She didn't do repeat performances, that was her golden rule, but, heavens above, she wanted him.

'Yours,' she murmured huskily. 'I share with Evie.'

He held her gaze for a moment before opening the door for her and following her to the lift. They rode it to the ninth floor in silence, Luca propped against one wall, staring across at Mia propped against the opposite wall. The bold way she returned his gaze tugged at his groin and his whole body tightened in anticipation.

Mia felt utterly dominated as Luca lounged against the wall, arms crossed. His gaze raked her body lingering on her breasts, her thighs, her boots. Then travelled all the way back up again to rest on her mouth.

The seconds ticked by as his eyes locked on her lips. Her tongue darted out to moisten them, a nervous gesture.

His nostrils flared. She swallowed.

His arms dropped. Her heart skipped a beat.

He took a step towards her. She tensed.

The lift dinged. He stopped. She breathed again.

'Ladies first,' he murmured. 'Number nineteen.'

Mia walked on legs made of Plasticine to the indicated apartment, aware of his eyes on her the whole time. She could barely breathe by the time she pulled up in front of his door.

Absently she reached for the doorhandle the same time he did. He sucked in a breath. 'Your hands are freezing,' he murmured.

'Yes,' she agreed. That was because all her blood had drained to her belly and breasts. In fact, apart from her torso she felt cold right through to her bones. She even shivered involuntarily.

Luca grinned at her as he pushed open the door. 'I have the perfect solution.'

He tugged on her hand and she followed him into the toasty centrally heated apartment.

Luca strode into his bedroom, Mia in tow, flipping lights on as he went. He walked straight past his bed, turning right into a spacious en suite. He ushered her in, shut the door, flipped on a wall-mounted heater, opened the shower screen and turned the hot tap on full bore. Instant heat puffed into the air from the shower head.

He turned to look at Mia, shrugging out of his jacket. 'Get naked.'

Mia quirked an eyebrow at his imperious command. 'Boy, you sure know how to seduce a woman.'

Luca grabbed her by her coat lapels and hauled her up against him. He lowered his mouth and on a groan unleashed a truly devastating kiss.

Mia's response was instantaneous. His mouth was hot, hot, hot and it fanned the flames burning in her belly to the rest of her body. Raising herself on tiptoe, she tunnelled her hands into his hair, pressed her breasts hard against the solid warmth of his chest.

His hands cupped her bottom, dragging their hips into alignment. Mia rubbed herself against him, causing a delicious friction that spread more warmth to every part of her body.

Luca groped for the tie of her coat and yanked it loose, his hands invading the cocoon of heat around her belly and stroking down her sides and back. He felt for her zip and undid it, pushing the skirt off her hips.

Mia broke away from the drugging intensity of his

mouth, her rough breath almost as loud as the teeming shower that poured an endless supply of steam into the hothouse atmosphere.

She was hot now. Very, very hot.

She quickly stepped out of her skirt, removed her jacket and followed it with her skivvy.

Luca's breath caught in his throat as she stood before him in matching champagne-coloured underwear and a pair of black knee-high boots.

He breathed out reverentially. '*Mia bella*,' he murmured. Thoughts of the mess he'd left behind in Marsala were now a distant memory.

Mia blushed. She had no idea what that meant but it sounded pretty damn complimentary to her. Which spurred her on even more. Removing the clasp from her hair, she shook it free so it fell down her back and flowed over her shoulders in a golden stream.

Aware that Luca, hands on hips, was watching her every move between heavy eyelids, she lifted a booted foot and placed it on the edge of the bath. She leaned forward until her breasts were brushing her thigh and slowly—very, very slowly—undid the side zipper on her boots.

Luca heard every one of the zip teeth release as he watched Mia intently. She had her back to him and his gaze roved hungrily over the brief triangle of fabric encasing the enticing wiggle of her butt cheeks. He lifted it higher to the indentation that formed the small of her back. Higher still to the long delicate stretch of her spine partially obscured by her long blonde tresses.

Mia looked over her shoulder at him and smiled as she straightened and flicked the boot off. The steam was building in the bathroom and her face felt flushed, although the kick in her pulse told her it had more to do with Luca's smouldering look than the atmospheric conditions.

When she turned back to bend over the other boot, Luca couldn't hold back. He moved in close behind her, pushing her hair off one shoulder and leaning forward to drop a kiss. His hands gripped her hips and pulled her against him, snuggling her bottom into the heat of his groin.

Luca was consumed with the erotic image in front of him. He fully clothed, his erection straining for release, Mia scantily clad and bent provocatively in front of him. He wanted to tear her knickers off and take her right here and now.

He pulled her in tight.

Mia's hand faltered on the zip as Luca circled his hips against her. She shut her eyes as he created delicious havoc in just the right spot, her breath coming faster. The boot forgotten, one foot still propped on the bath edge, she straightened, arching her back against him, her arms snaking up behind her to clasp around his neck, gratified to feel both of his hands slide up from her hips, over her belly and higher.

'Mia,' he groaned into her ear as his hands found her satin-clad breasts.

Mia whimpered, biting her lip as he squeezed and flattened then peeled the cups aside and ran the pads of his thumbs against her tight, bare nipples.

'I want to be inside you,' he murmured, his lips finding her neck and licking all the sensitive areas.

Mia opened her mouth to answer but one of his hands moved lower and dipped beneath the band of her underwear, seeking the slick heat of her. He ploughed a finger through her aching sex and found just the right spot, causing her to lose all vocal ability.

'Mia,' he murmured as she bucked against him. 'You are hot here. Very, very hot.'

Mia couldn't speak as one hand teased a nipple and the other moved rhythmically between her thighs. Her knee buckled slightly and she was vaguely aware of Luca pulling her back against him.

Her hands, however, had a mind of their own and while she left one anchored around his neck the other one sought to touch him as intimately as he was touching her.

She reached behind her, grabbing for his belt as her brain liquefied. One-handed and on an inexorable march towards orgasm, she managed the buckle and the zip and finally she was freeing him, his hard length surging into her palm.

Luca threw his head back on a groan, squeezing his eyes shut as she gripped him firmly and ran her hand up and down the length of him. The urge to bury himself in her, ram into all that slick heat as far as he could go, roared through him as his fingers picked up their pace.

Mia could feel the edges of her world starting to fray and she gripped his neck hard as a wild heat started to boil out of control in the deepest part of her. Her hand clamped around his girth became dysfunctional and un-coordinated as the all-consuming urge to ride his finger, seek her own pleasure, became a blinding imperative.

She sagged against him as standing upright became impossible. 'Luca,' she moaned.

'Yes,' he whispered in her ear. 'Yes.'

'Luca-a-a-a!'

She bucked as the orgasm slammed into her. It picked her up, whirled her round and smashed her back down only to lift her again—higher. She gasped and jerked against him, rocking her pelvis in sync with his fingers, squeezing every last liquid drop of pleasure out of it.

'Yes, Mia, yes,' he urged, rubbing harder and faster, pushing a finger deep inside her, feeling her clamp hard around him.

Mia moaned loudly as her body automatically accepted his penetration. It was shockingly satisfying and she cried out as another finger filled her.

Luca held her tight against him as she whimpered and gyrated her pelvis, grinding herself against the hard intrusion of his fingers.

The orgasm began to fade and Mia felt as if she was walking through a rainbow. Cool mists of colour stroked her skin like sighs, caressing and cradling, bringing her down gently despite the frantic beat of her heart and the tortured sound of her breath.

Finally her feet touched the ground and she opened her eyes. Became aware that she was leaning heavily into Luca, his hands were cradling her hips and his erection still coursed hard and potent in her hand.

She moved against him. Dropped her leg to the floor, kicked off her boot and turned in his arms.

Luca brushed her hair off her shoulder. 'Warm now?' He grinned.

Mia laughed. A part of her was vaguely aware the floor tiles were warm underfoot and that he could obviously afford to fork out for one of the more luxuriously appointed apartments. And that he no doubt had Bridge and Opera house views too.

But none of that mattered as she plastered her lips

to his. It only mattered that she could make him groan just like that. And…she rubbed herself along the length of him…hard just like this.

'Shower,' she murmured, pulling back and quickly divesting herself of her underwear before stepping into the spacious cubicle.

She turned through the cloud of steam. 'Are you coming?' she asked.

Luca, captivated by the water running over her naked body and her hair turning dark gold as the spray doused it, didn't move for a moment.

'Luca,' Mia growled impatiently, taking in his partially undressed body and his very, very aroused state. 'Come here and do me against the tiles.'

Her provocative words galvanised him into action and he tore at his shirt, toeing off his shoes, grabbing for his wallet before he divested himself of his trousers, pulling out a foil packet, ripping it open and hastily donning the protection he never went without.

Two steps and he was in a cloud of steam, enveloped by hot water and her. He plastered her against the requested wall and plundered her lips and her neck and her breasts with his mouth. Then he boosted her up the tiles, positioned her slippery body at just the right height and plunged straight into her, his mouth swallowing her guttural cry.

Luca pounded into her relentlessly, satisfied to hear her gasps, to see the loll of her head as each thrust rocked her entire body. He tongued her breasts, her heat and her sweat and her essence in each drop of water sluicing over her nipples.

Pressure built strongly and relentlessly as each drive took him closer. In his veins, in his head, in his loins.

Pleasure, so intense it hurt, coiled low in his gut. She cried out and bucked in his arms and the coil whipped out, cracking like a lightning strike, zapping every erogenous zone, every cell.

She tightened around him and he came and he came and he came.

Luca was in the kitchen, percolating coffee in nothing but a low-slung towel, when Mia came out of the bathroom dressed in the clothes she'd arrived in half an hour earlier.

Minus her underwear.

And the earring she'd lost somewhere in the midst of the head-banging sex. Down the drainhole, she suspected. Her hair was hanging in wet strips down her back and her body ached all over.

In a good way.

'Coffee?' he asked.

Mia shook her head, distracted by the perfection of him. Broad shoulders, trim hips, flat belly. His damp hair curled around his nape and ears. She felt the slight ache inside her begin to throb in carnal recognition of him and the things he could do.

It'd be so easy to take four or five paces forward and whip that towel away. Drop to her knees. Show him she was a pretty dab hand at doling out pleasure too. Go again right there on the kitchen floor as her traitorous body was demanding.

But then what? Once more after that? Stay the night?

She wasn't a stay-the-night kind of girl. It was why she always went to the guy's place—easier to leave and never look back than to tell someone to go.

'No, thanks,' she murmured. 'I'm going to head home.'

Luca lounged against the bench and crossed his arms over his very impressive chest. 'You're not clingy. I like that.'

Mia nodded. 'Good. Looks like we'll get along just fine, then.'

'I think you're the first woman I've met who didn't want to be held afterwards.'

Mia shook her head. 'Not the cuddling type, I'm afraid.'

Luca regarded her silently for a few moments. He could almost buy into her act. Except he'd seen another side to her that first night. Sure, Mia McKenzie seemed feisty and tough but there was definitely a vulnerable side.

She was an intriguing woman.

'And why is that?' Luca mused.

Mia knew exactly why. She wasn't blind to the scars that growing up in an emotionally barren house had left. Sex was a quick, easy connection—she'd found that out at uni. But cuddling—staying?—was hard. Sex was physically intimate. Cuddles emotionally intimate. Certainly not something she'd had an awful lot of experience with from the main male role model in her life as she'd been growing up.

Cuddles called for a certain level of trust. And she'd been too scarred to trust anyone at any level—particularly men.

He was standing patiently, all big and solid, looking at her with expectation. She could have easily opened her mouth and told him the reasons.

But it was none of his damn business.

'It sends the wrong message,' she said.

Mia shifted slightly as Luca studied her with his big brown eyes. It was kind of unnerving.

She straightened her shoulders. 'Do you have a problem with that?'

Like she cared if he did.

Luca stayed very still. 'No. It just seems like something a—'

'What?' she interrupted, scorn lacing her voice as her blood pressure rose a couple of notches. 'A man? Like something a man would say?'

Why was it okay for men to use women for sex but not for women to use men?

'It's a new century, Luca. Gotta move with the times.'

Luca chuckled at the sudden glint of fire in her stained-glass eyes. Her whole body had become animated. His gaze drifted to the bounce of her unfettered breasts before it flicked back to her face. 'Sicilian men aren't known for their tendency to move with the times.'

Mia shoved her hands on her hips as her nipples responded to his blatant stare. 'You going to go all Neanderthal on me, Luca?'

Luca pushed off the bench and moved towards her. 'Not at all. I am a highly evolved Sicilian. I like a woman who knows what she wants.'

Mia watched him prowl closer and felt that ache intensify. How was it possible to look sexy and menacing all at the same time?

He stopped in front of her, close, nearly touching. But not. 'Especially one who appreciates the type of liaisons I also happen to favour.' He dropped his gaze to her mouth for long moments before returning it to her face. 'Where have you been all my life?' He grinned.

It took Mia a moment to reel her body in enough to respond. Kissing him seemed the best course of action but she needed to go home.

She. Must. Go. Home.

And never come back.

Mia took a step back. 'Goodnight, Luca. See you in the morning.'

Luca watched the sway of her hips as she made her way to the door and felt himself twitch beneath the towel. 'I'm having a party in a couple of weeks. Everyone from work is coming. You should too.'

Mia's hand paused on the doorknob. 'No,' she said, without looking back.

One thing she knew for sure was that Luca wasn't like any other man she'd known. In a brief time he'd got firmly under her skin and she wasn't about to lose the upper hand to him.

There wouldn't be a next time. Certainly not a party.

Luca's wicked chuckle mocked her as she turned the handle and slipped out of the apartment.

Evie bustled through the deserted outpatients department at seven o'clock the next evening. She'd begged a chart from Enid Kenny, the NUM of the department earlier, who'd relinquished it only after Evie had promised faithfully to personally return it before she left for the day.

Someone else might have sent a courier but not Evie. Sister Enid Kenny was an institution around The Harbour and not to be messed with! Hence the sweet note and box of chocolates she was also clutching in her hand.

She turned right, passing a row of examination rooms

on her way to Enid's office. She noticed a light on in the far office. Voices floated out. Male voices. She frowned. Who on earth was working this late?

Then, to her utter surprise, Finn stepped out, followed by Rupert Davidson. Evie faltered and dived into the nearest exam room. Recovering quickly, she cautiously peeked around the door. In the empty department their voices carried easily and she eavesdropped unashamedly.

She watched as they shook hands and Rupert said, 'You're entitled to a second opinion, Finn. But you know as well as I do that the conservative approach is only a sticky plaster and you can't keep going on like this. Surgery will have to happen at some stage.'

Then Finn nodded but even from a few metres away she could see that familiar set to his unshaven jaw. 'Thanks, Rupert. I'll think about it.'

And then he turned and walked away in the opposite direction.

Evie fell back against the wall of the examination room, her heart pounding. What the hell had that been about? She grappled with what she'd heard and seen, trying to make sense of it.

Finn was seeing Rupert? A neurologist? *You can't keep going on like this.* Was there something wrong?

She recalled the uneasy feelings she'd had for a while now that something was up with Finn, and the rumours that he'd been wounded on a tour in Afghanistan when he'd been in the army. Had he sustained injuries during his time there? Injuries that could affect his job?

Eric Frobisher, SHH's officious medical director, would be furious if that was the case. He and Finn already butted heads on a regular basis.

Evie drummed her fingers against the chart as curiosity and concern for Finn warred within her. She told herself it was pure collegial interest. One doctor looking out for another. Even if said doctor was the most surly and unappreciative man she'd ever met.

Making a decision, Evie waited for a couple of minutes before pushing herself off the wall and heading towards her original destination. She stopped in midstride as she passed the last office and blinked at Rupert with what she hoped was her very best round-eyed surprise.

'Rupert?' she asked. 'What are you still doing here? Burning the candle at both ends?'

Rupert, who was writing in a chart, laughed as he put down his pen. 'No such luck. Just a late appointment.'

Evie nodded, glancing at the chart trying to see a name. 'Gosh, that's dedication.' She smiled.

Rupert shrugged. 'It was a favour.' He nodded at the package in her hand. 'What about you? Those chocolates for me?'

She laughed. 'Oh, no, these are major sucking-up chocolates for Enid.'

Rupert laughed back. 'You're coming to Luca's party in a couple of weeks?' she asked.

Rupert nodded. 'Wouldn't miss it for the world.'

'Great,' she said as she backed out the door, her head still swimming with what she'd just witnessed.

What in the hell was wrong with Finn Kennedy?

CHAPTER FIVE

Two weeks later Mia was watching the clock, thinking that for once in her working life she might actually get off on time. Her shift, one of those rare short shifts, was due to finish at two and things were looking good. With Evie going off to Luca's party tonight—the one she was *not* going to attend, no matter how much Evie begged—she had a quiet night of reading planned.

The latest blockbuster novel had been sitting on her bedside table, gathering dust, for too long.

She glanced nervously over at the man in question as he spoke on the phone at the other end of the central monitoring station. She'd managed to keep her attraction at bay this past fortnight—until last night. A cluttered, semi-dark storeroom had seriously tried her resolve to keep away when they'd both ended up inside. His body had been big and close, his lips had kicked up into a frank smile, his gaze firmly fixed on her mouth.

How she hadn't pushed him against the wall and ravaged him she still wasn't sure.

But she hadn't. She'd caught herself at the last second. Remembered that she'd already broken her golden rule once and she wasn't going to do it again. Even if he was the most skilled, most exciting lover she'd ever known.

Unfortunately, the buzz from last night's near kiss was still vibrating through her system and they'd been trading furtive glances all morning. He'd looked at her with undiluted lust half an hour ago and she still could barely see straight.

His gaze met hers again, his brown eyes knowing, and her pulse picked up a notch.

'Ambulance two minutes out.'

The urgent note in Nola's voice dragged her attention back to reality and Mia looked down to where the efficient triage nurse sat, the red emergency phone to her ear, speaking out loud as she wrote the details down from the ambulance coms centre.

'Thirty-year-old male. Jumper. Two storeys. Bilateral comminuted fractured tib and fibs, right compound fractured femur, query fractured pelvis, query spinal injuries, fractured right ribs, GCS twelve, major internal injuries, query ruptured spleen, hypotensive and tachycardic.'

Luca joined them, all business now as he read the details again over Nola's shoulder.

'I'll page Ortho and General Surgery,' Mia said, grabbing the phone nearest her as the distant wail of a siren permeated the thick walls of the hospital.

Luca also picked up a phone. 'I'll alert blood bank that we might need to initiate the massive transfusion protocol.'

By the time the ambulance pulled up a minute later, everything was prepped and Luca and Mia were standing outside, ready to receive the patient.

Luca grabbed the ambulance doorhandle and pulled

it open as the paramedic driving the vehicle joined them, launching into a rapid-fire handover of injuries, actual and suspected.

He and the treating paramedic pulled the gurney out of the back of the ambulance. The patient was moaning, his face covered by an oxygen mask.

'Pupils equal and reacting,' the paramedica continued as they pushed the gurney towards the entrance, Mia and Luca keeping pace. 'BP ninety over sixty, pulse one hundred and forty, resps fifty and shallow. Right chest tube inserted on scene, two IV cannulae wide open.'

'Do we know what happened?' Mia asked, clinging to the gurney rail as they practically flew inside to the prepared trauma cubicle.

'Paternity test showed he wasn't the baby's daddy,' the paramedic stated dispassionately.

Mia felt a prickle up her spine as she and Luca shared a look. 'Is his name Stan?' she asked.

The paramedic nodded. 'Stanley James.'

Repeat customers—especially suicides attempts— were reasonably common in the department. As were frequent-flyer drug addicts and patients with chronic conditions. Mia treated them all with courtesy and professionalism, careful not to get emotionally invested in them.

But this man had held her at knifepoint. Had yanked her back into the convoluted emotions of her childhood. Had been the catalyst for what had happened later that night with Luca.

Mia felt sick as two nurses descended and between the four of them they quickly transferred Stan to the hospital gurney on the count of three. Whether she liked it or not, she and Stanley were connected.

And she really didn't want to have to deal with that.

Stan pulled his mask off and grabbed her hand. 'I told you,' he said. 'I told you she was cheating on me.'

Mia looked into his anguished face, trying not to see her father, trying only to see the man who had menaced her with a knife. But he looked…broken.

Just like her father.

'It's going to be okay, Stan,' she murmured, replacing his mask as people bustled around her. 'We're going to get you patched up.'

He pulled it off again. 'No. Just leave me. Just leave me to die.'

Mia and Luca's gazes met for a moment. She felt rage build inside as she looked back down at Stan. He'd taken the coward's way out, just like her father. Her father had walked, Stan had jumped—both ways showed very little regard for the people left behind.

For a tiny baby. For a bewildered ten-year-old girl.

'Please, just let me die,' Stan begged.

Mia bit down on the urge to tell Stan that if he'd really wanted to die he should have jumped from a higher building. The fact that he hadn't spoke volumes about the incident. She doubted it was a true attempt—more like a cry for help.

And she was damned if she was going to let him die on her watch.

She put the mask back. 'Can't do that, I'm afraid, Stan.'

'We need X-Ray,' Luca said. 'And get Psych down here. I want to consult with John Allen.'

Luca and Mia, their personal situation forgotten,

worked methodically over the next hour to stabilise Stan for Theatre. They intubated, placed lines and another chest tube, gave blood and plasma expanders, consulted with Ortho, General Surgery and Radiology.

And all the time Luca was chanting, *Come on, Stan, come on Stan, come on Stan. Don't die. Don't die. Don't die.* If it took everything he had, Luca was not going to let this man die.

Not that he'd ever been particularly emotional about life-and-death situations. Being a trauma specialist, he saw the struggle between the two on a regular basis. Like two powerfully competing forces pulling in opposite directions. He worked hard to save every patient but not even he was arrogant enough to assume that hard work was always enough.

Sometimes, no matter what he threw at a patient, they died.

He got that. People died.

Children, teenagers, athletes, mothers, forty-year-olds with everything to live for.

People died.

Hell…they were all dying.

But the truth was, Stan had struck a chord. And probably for the first time ever he actually felt personally invested in a patient. And not because Stan had threatened him with a knife but because Luca knew all about the demons that had driven him.

He knew how it felt to be betrayed by the person you loved. How it felt to have your whole world yanked out from under you. And how life-changing that could be.

He knew how it felt to be a father one moment and then suddenly not.

To feel powerless.

To feel alone.

It may have been a whole bunch of years ago but some things never left you.

He glanced at Mia as she took a phone call from the lab. Mia, who was working just as hard to pull Stan through. The man who had threatened to stab her, who had slashed her arm with a knife.

What was driving her?

The same things that had driven her to cry out in her sleep that night? That had spurred her to seek amnesia in his arms?

What were the things that haunted her? That made her tough and feisty and not the *cuddling* type?

Had Stan stirred them up for her as he had stirred things up from *his* past? *Daddy, come back.* That's what she'd cried out that night. Did Stan remind her of her father as he had reminded him of his sixteen-year-old self?

'Haemoglobin's eight,' Mia announced. She ordered another bag of blood to be hung and administered stat. 'Let's get him to Theatre for that laparotomy,' she said. 'He's bleeding from somewhere.'

As if by magic, an anaesthetist, a nurse and two orderlies arrived and Luca dragged himself out of his reverie to help with the handover.

Within ten minutes Stan had been whisked away and the two of them stood in an empty trauma bay. The floor was littered with packaging and discarded dressing material that had fallen short of the bin. And where there'd been frantic activity and the beeps and alarms of monitors seconds ago, there was now absolute quiet.

Luca glanced at Mia watching Stan disappear down

the corridor with a look on her face he couldn't quite
work out.

He put his arm around her shoulder. 'He'll be okay,'
he said, even though he had no earthly idea why he'd
said it and absolutely no way of knowing how true it
was.

Mia nodded. Physically, sure…maybe. After an extended recovery period and if they could control the
bleeding and get him through about a hundred compli-
cations that could arise.

But mentally?

Would Stan ever be the same again? Was her father?

For a few insane seconds she leaned into the hug,
soaking up the comfort, surprised to find that she
needed it as a block of unexpected emotion lodged in
her chest, invading her throat, threatening to choke her.

And she hated it.

She pulled away, stripped off her plastic gown and
peeled off her gloves, disposing of them in an overflow-
ing bin.

'I'll follow up with John,' she said.

And left Luca behind in the bay.

Later that evening, Mia accompanied Evie to the party.
She'd finally caved to her friend's relentless insistence
that she go. Stan's case had been playing on her mind all
afternoon and she knew she wouldn't be able to settle
to a book. She needed a distraction and there was no
doubt Luca distracted the hell out of her.

That brief comforting hug had been playing on her
mind too but she pushed it aside. The distraction she
needed from Luca did not involve anything as nurtur-

ing as comfort. She needed hard and ready. Hot and sweaty. Down and dirty.

And since she knew he gave it better than anyone else—could obliterate everything else from her brain—only he would do.

The party was in full swing when they finally stepped inside two hours late. Familiar faces milled in groups all around Luca's apartment and greeted them enthusiastically, despite their tardiness. Shift workers accepted that shift times varied and punctuality was fluid.

Mia felt Luca's eyes on her instantly and looked directly at him. Neither of them smiled as music pulsed around them and their gazes ate each other up.

Luca, surprised to see her, devoured the sight of her as she shrugged out of her leather jacket and made her way over to Luke Williams, one of The Harbour's plastic surgeons specialising in burns, and his partner, Lily, a nurse at SHH.

Mia was wearing a tight denim skirt that didn't quite reach her knees, a pair of long rainbow-striped socks that ended in little bows just below her knees and a singlet-style shirt that did up snugly across her front with corset-style lacing.

Thank goodness his apartment was centrally heated.

Her hair hung loose around her shoulders and an image of him removing that lacing with his teeth surrounded by the curtain of her golden hair wreaked havoc in his groin.

His gaze drifted to the reddish-pink scar on her upper arm visible from all the way across the room. It reminded him of that night and what had happened.

It reminded him of today. Of anguish so familiar he

had recognised it immediately. Of those brief few seconds with Mia after Stan had left for Theatre when he'd felt a strange moment of solidarity, of connection.

He pushed the thought aside. Stan had made it out of surgery and was stable in Intensive Care. And Mia had stepped away from him.

Work was work.

This was a party.

He took a swig out of his long-necked beer, his eyes never leaving her. She laughed at something Luke said and shook her head, her hair swinging enticingly around the cleavage barely contained by the faux corset top.

She glanced at him and their gazes locked, the message in her eyes heating his loins. He took another pull from his beer, keeping up the eye contact, matching her frank, unwavering stare. If she wanted to play chicken, he was up for it. He smiled to himself as Lily said something to her and Mia was forced to break contact first.

Why had she come when she'd been so adamant she wouldn't?

Just for the sex she was patently up for? Or was there something more to it? Had Stan rattled her again? Or maybe that moment they'd shared had? Had she come to prove it hadn't? Or to explore if it had?

The thought alarmed him and Luca served himself up a mental slap. What the hell business was it of his? Her motivations? He knew what he wanted and it didn't involve second-guessing a gorgeous woman who had come here to have sex with him. Whatever she was offering, he was going to take it.

And have a damn fine time doing so.

* * *

Mia wandered around the different groups of people, stopping to chat, talk shop, laugh with her friends and colleagues. And all the time she was conscious of Luca tracking her around the room. He hadn't even said hello to her but she could sense his intense interest, feel the weight of his gaze, the heat of his laser-like focus trained squarely on her back.

Sure, he was playing the perfect host—attentive and charming as he moved around the apartment—but underneath that bronzed Latin skin she could sense the leashed desire he was just barely keeping a lid on. His glances may be smouldering with lust but she could also feel his impatience as they slowly circled each other.

She walked past a large bay window and stopped to admire the view. She knew he'd have one. A man with heated bathroom tiles would certainly have a view!

The iron arch of the illuminated Sydney Harbour Bridge and the floodlit white sails of the Opera House glowed like beacons in the night. Of course, these could also be seen from the upper floors of SHH but it was still a pretty amazing sight, no matter how many times she'd been privy to it.

The hairs on the back of her neck prickled and she was instantly aware he was zeroing in.

Luca sauntered up to her. 'I didn't think you were coming,' he murmured.

Mia didn't turn to look at him. She could see his reflection. Tall, broad shouldered, looking very fine in snug blue jeans and a close-fitting black T-shirt.

All he needed was *Security* emblazoned across the front. Or maybe *Italian Stallion.*

'Nice view.'

Luca, who hadn't taken his eyes of her said, 'Indeed.'

He took a sip of his beer. 'The view from my bedroom is even better.'

Mia smiled. 'Don't you have guests to entertain?'

Luca chuckled, turning so his back was to the window. Their arms brushed and he felt a kick in his groin. 'They seem to be amusing themselves just fine.'

Mia turned too just in time to see Finn entering with a stunning-looking redhead she'd not seen before.

'I didn't think Finn would come,' she mused. Evie had been sure of it but she herself hadn't been convinced.

'Why not?' Luca frowned.

'He's not really the social type.'

He shrugged. 'He is tonight.'

Apparently. Very social, if the redhead's relaxed intimacy was anything to go by. Mia flicked a glance towards Evie and watched her friend's face fall a little. She gave an inward sigh, wishing she understood Evie's attraction to the maverick surgeon.

Sure, his legendary status was alluring and he was sexy in a rumpled kind of way. And single. But that just-rolled-out-of-bed look didn't do it for her.

She preferred clean-shaven men.

Like the one standing beside her.

'So...' Luca dropped his head so his mouth was near her ear. 'About that view?'

Mia felt goose-bumps break out on her arms as her belly constricted. But Evie was looking around with an overly bright smile on her face and Mia knew that her friend needed her.

'Patience is a virtue,' she murmured.

She heard Luca chuckling as she slunk away.

* * *

Half an hour later Evie was standing in a circle, ostensibly talking to Mia, Luke Williams and a couple of nurses from the emergency department. But her gaze kept wandering to Finn, who was sitting on the wide windowsill of the bay window, talking to Rupert. He had dismissed the redhead when Rupert had approached and now they seemed to be having quite an intense discussion.

Finn was nursing his usual Scotch and it didn't look like he appreciated what Rupert had to say. After another minute Rupert shrugged and walked away.

'Excuse me, guys. I'll go and grab another drink.'

She felt Mia's concerned gaze on her as she slipped away but no one else paid any attention. Evie grabbed a beer out of the ice-filled sink then wended her way through to Finn.

Finn watched Evie approach through the prism of his glass. She lifted a beer bottle to her lips and tipped her head back as she drew close. When she was done her lips were moist and he found himself wondering what she tasted like.

He tensed at the errant thought, which cranked up the throb in his already aching arm. That, on top of Rupert's little chat, made him even crankier.

'Well, well, well. I thought the Lockheart heiress would be into champagne.'

Evie let the insult slide off her back. She'd learned to chug beer and drink shots at uni just to annoy her parents.

'Beer is better.'

She stood in front of him, one hand shoved into the front pocket of her skinny jeans, the other one wrapped around the bottle. She was wearing a floaty top that fell off her shoulder, which he studiously ignored.

He raised his glass to the light. 'Scotch is the only drink.' It smoothed out the edges and helped with the pain. Physical and mental.

Evie inspected him. Sprawled on the windowsill, his shaggy look was sexy as hell. Unlike other guys she knew, the stubble was real, hinting at disregard rather than fashion. It also lent authenticity to the boast she'd once overheard—apparently he only ever got three or four hours' sleep a night.

She shook her head. *Why?* Was it deliberate? Did his brilliant mind never shut off or was it involuntary? Was the mysterious injury responsible for Finn's chronic insomnia? Or had his time in the army left him with nightmares? It was rumoured he'd been to Afghanistan and Iraq.

Or was it just the redhead or any of the other women he was seen with, keeping him up all night?

She didn't understand why she felt so compelled to try and figure him out. But she did. 'What did Rupert want?'

Finn, the glass halfway to his mouth, paused slightly before lifting it to his lips and draining the entire glass.

'I need another drink,' he said.

'I heard you and Rupert talking a couple of weeks ago. It was in the evening…in the outpatients department.'

Finn felt his hackles rise. 'Spying for Daddy?' He knew how chummy the hospital's biggest benefactor was with pernickety Eric Frobisher.

Evie heard the low menace in his voice and watched as his piercing blue eyes practically bored into her.

'He mentioned surgery.' Evie paused and perused his hard, shuttered face for any signs of softening. 'Is there something wrong, Finn?'

Finn heard the quiet strength in her voice. As if it never occurred to her that he wouldn't confess. The kind of strength that came from growing up in a nurturing environment where a person's opinion, even a child's, mattered.

'I think you should stick with diagnosing complex heart conditions.'

She ploughed on despite his rigid jaw and frigid stare. 'There are rumours about you being wounded in the army. Do you have some residual effects from that?'

Finn's heart pounded in his chest. Only little Miss Rich Girl would dare to push him like this. He stood, instantly towering over her, and was gratified to see her take a step back, to see she wasn't so sure of herself after all. 'I need a drink.'

He brushed past her without looking back.

Conversation over.

At two am only Mia and Evie remained as Luca shut his door on the last of his guests. He caught Mia's eye. She'd been a walking, talking temptation all night and now it was time to pay the piper.

Mia grinned at him. 'I'm going to stay and help Luca clean up,' she said to Evie, carrying some glasses into the kitchen and setting them on the substantial granite bench top beside the sink.

Evie nodded, tired after her long day shift and distracted by thoughts of Finn, who had hastily downed a drink after their *chat* then left with the redhead clinging to his arm. 'I'll help.'

Luca, picking up some more glasses behind where Evie was located, shook his head and mouthed, 'No.'

Mia grinned some more. 'No, Evie. You're done in. Go to bed. I won't be far behind you.' She was so revved up she'd probably come in under a minute.

'Oh, but—'

'No buts,' Luca insisted. 'Go. We'll be fine.'

Evie *was* exhausted. 'Well…if you're sure…?'

Luca nodded, vigorously aware that Mia had turned on the tap and was leaning over the sink. 'Absolutely.'

He ushered Evie out the door and shut it with quiet determination then leant against it, hard. He watched Mia fill the sink with glassware through a haze of high-octane lust.

'Leave that,' he said as he slowly prowled towards her.

Mia looked at him and grinned. It faded in a flash at the naked intent in his gaze. 'It's just a few dishes,' she said lamely as her insides melted to the consistency of chocolate sauce.

Just like his lust-drunk eyes.

Luca reached her side, flicked off the tap, swept the remaining dirty dishes into the sink with a huge clatter, grabbed her around the waist and boosted her up onto the bench.

Mia opened her mouth to protest against the tinkling glass and chipping crockery but mostly the cold granite on the backs of her legs. But Luca didn't give her a chance. He stepped between her thighs, forcing them apart, and claimed her mouth in a kiss that silenced all her inane worries.

A kiss that lit a fuse that ignited a powder keg. After

two weeks of abstinence and an evening of sexual chess they devoured each other like a raging bushfire.

Luca slipped his hands under the hem of her skirt, pushing it up her thighs, exposing her flesh and her heat. He dragged her core hard against him, the bench top just the right height, moaning when Mia locked her ankles around his waist, wedging them together as intimately as they could be fully clothed. She gasped as he kissed down her neck—hard, biting kisses that stiffened her nipples to unbearable points.

Yes. This was what she needed.

This.

Something to forget the day.

She grabbed for the snap on his jeans as he squeezed a breast with his hand. She undid his zip, pushed his underwear aside and grasped his warm velvet girth.

His mouth slammed against hers on a full, throaty groan as he fumbled with the lacing of her shirt, half undoing, half tearing at the fabric until it succumbed to his will. He dragged his mouth from hers, down, down, down to her breasts, ripping aside the cups of her transparent bra and gorging on the ripeness of her nipples.

Mia's back arched, one hand automatically holding his head to her, the other squeezing his rampant erection, rubbing herself against it, whimpering as it caused the most wicked friction.

'Back pocket,' Luca whispered as he lifted his head to pay equal homage to her other breast.

Mia fumbled. His lips were creating havoc and she felt like she'd been to the dentist and been given a full body shot.

Limp with lust. Prostrate with pleasure.

Her fingers found the hard edges of foil and whipped

it out triumphantly as his hand pushed aside her undies and stroked against her so intimately she thought she was going to die.

Too much more of that and she'd be done.

It was bloody-mindedness alone that accomplished sheathing him as he sought and found where she was hottest. Where she was the most ready.

'Ah,' she cried as the friction hit just the right spot. 'Now,' she cried, tilting her pelvis in supplication. 'Now.'

Luca didn't need a translation. He ran his palms up her back, anchored both hands over her shoulders, leaned forward to suck hard on a ripe, plump, moist nipple and rammed into her in one quick decisive thrust of his hips.

Their combined groan no doubt caused a blip at some seismic centre somewhere.

And then they were moving and pounding together in unison, rocking and rocking, higher and higher, gasping and sighing and reaching for breath until it all coalesced in one magical moment and the stars shattered around them.

CHAPTER SIX

A WEEK later Mia was examining a severe case of cellulitis around a ten-day-old calf laceration when Luca entered the cubicle. He smiled at her and her breath hitched.

'Can I help you, Dr di Angelo?'

'You don't happen to have an otoscope by any chance? They all seem to have gone walking.'

Mia didn't register his words. Just the way his eyes crinkled at the edges as he looked at her with a gaze that paid way too much attention to the dip of her cleavage. And the way his lips moved, all soft and full, exactly the same as when they stroked down her neck.

Luca quirked an eyebrow as Mia's normally clear blue gaze became a little heated. 'Mia?'

She blinked and her cheeks warmed as she realised she had no idea what he'd asked for. 'Sorry?'

Luca grinned. It wasn't often he saw her blush and he liked it. It seemed completely at odds with her feisty, my-way-or-the-highway demeanour, softening her. Cranking up the strong sense of attraction another notch. 'Otoscope?'

'Oh. Yes.' she shook her head to clear it as she removed the equipment from the pocket she'd jammed it in earlier. 'Here.'

Their fingers brushed as he took it and Luca smiled again as he felt the pulse of awareness in his fingertips and knew she'd felt it too. 'Thank you.'

It took Mia a few seconds to realise he'd disappeared as her body recovered from just the faintest contact with his.

'He's a bit of a hottie, dear.'

Mia looked down absently at Mable Richardson, her eighty-six-year-old patient. She had snowy white hair and a wicked gleam in her eyes.

'He could park his slippers under my bed any day.' Mable sighed. 'If I was only forty years younger...'

Mia stared at her patient open-mouthed, shocked by such ribald frankness from an octogenarian.

Mable cackled. 'I'm old, deary, not dead.'

Mia laughed. From the twinkle in her eyes, Mable was obviously one of those lovely old ladies who loved to shock.

'Laugh all you want.' Mable patted Mia's hand. 'You blink one day and suddenly you're eighty-six. Mark my words, young lady—take your opportunities when you get them.' And then she winked.

'Mable, you're incorrigible.'

Mable cackled again, seemingly delighted by Mia's description. 'I hope so, deary.'

Mia returned her attention to Mable's gardening wound, which had developed an infection in the sub-cutaneous tissues. Had Mable seen something pass between her and Luca—something intangible—that had prompted such an observation, or was she just someone who appreciated good eye candy when she saw it?

Not for the first time she wondered what the hell she and Luca were doing. Okay, there'd been no more liaisons since the party and they'd only been together a few times anyway. But it was a few times more than she'd ever allowed any other man. And, if his rep was accurate, the same applied to him.

Why did this man, Luca di Angelo of all men, have this…pull, this sway over her?

No.

Mia smiled absently at Mable as she pulled the gurney rail up decisively and excused herself to arrange for Mable's admission for several days of intravenous antibiotics.

She wasn't going to analyse what had gone on.

She wasn't going to give it any importance by pontificating over it.

They were attracted to each other. They'd had a good time. And that was that.

Period.

A couple of hours later the red emergency phone rang and Luca picked it up. He scribbled notes as he listened to the ambulance comms officer on the other end.

Mia and Evie looked at him as he hung up and Mia quirked an eyebrow. 'Multiple casualties, first five minutes out, from the Douglas army base. Some sort of an explosion. Two critical. One with penetrating chest trauma, the other with a partially severed leg.'

Caroline, on triage, appeared at his elbow and said, 'On it.'

Luca thanked her. 'I'll page Finn,' he said.

Then everyone scattered to do their jobs, ensuring the trauma bays were fully stocked for the incoming wounded and other departments alerted, including Pathology, Radiology and the operating theatres. Luckily it was Sunday when demand for these services was reduced.

Finn, in his standard surgical uniform of blue scrubs, arrived just as the first ambulance was pulling in.

'You take the chest trauma,' Luca said to his colleague, donning a yellow paper gown. 'I'll take the leg.'

Finn nodded, accepting a gown from Evie and quickly securing it before snapping disposable gloves into place.

'Evie, you go with Finn. Mia, you're with me.'

Finn opened his mouth to protest but Mia and Luca had already split off and ultimately it didn't matter who worked with him as long as they were competent. And, as reluctant as he had been to believe it, Princess Evie knew her stuff.

'You ready for this?' he demanded as the paramedic opened the back door.

Evie nodded, determined not to show him how much his enquiry rankled. 'Of course.' She gave him a serene smile to hide her gritted teeth.

A cry of pain, like that of a wounded animal, penetrated Finn's cynicism and tore his attention away to the soldier on the gurney, his dusty boots and army fatigues eerily familiar.

It took him back a lot of years.

He knew all about cries like that. Had heard them too often to forget. Had held Isaac, rocked him, as the yelling had quietened and finally abated, leaving only silence as the life had drained from his brother's trusting eyes.

'Twenty-eighty-year-old sergeant, bomb disposal

officer at Douglas, took the full impact of an explosive device. Safety gear rendered some protection.'

Finn shook his head and blinked as the rapid-fire handover spat out at him like the rat-a-tat of a machine gun. He couldn't think about Isaac. About a distant battlefield.

This soldier needed him.

But *this* soldier was about Isaac's age and cried out in pain just like Isaac had.

Finn pushed it away, knocked it back as the gurney moved rapidly into the emergency department.

'Matthew! Matthew!' the soldier called, pulling the oxygen mask aside with bloodied hands.

The paramedic continued his handover above the soldier's increasingly frantic cries. Evie listened intently while Finn stared at the young man's bloody face.

'Matty!'

'Matthew is his brother,' the paramedic informed Finn and Evie quietly as he helped transfer the soldier to the hospital gurney. 'He's the second soldier. With the…leg.'

Finn gave a grim nod as he looked at the blood-soaked combat shirt that had been cut away from the bleeding chest wound. Isaac had cried out for him, too. He could still hear the panic in his brother's voice. *Finn! Finn!*

'Matthew. Are you okay, Matthew?'

Finn moved in close to the soldier's head while all around him nurses jumped into action. Tears had cut grimy streaks through his grisly war paint of dirt and blood.

'Oxygen saturations eighty-nine, tachy at one fifty-nine,' a nurse relayed.

Finn's heart thundered in his chest as he fought back a tide of memories he'd thought he'd long ago buried deep. 'What's your name, Sergeant?'

Finn's enquiry was quiet but held a note of authority not forgotten from his own time in the army. It seemed to settle the soldier's agitation. He looked at Finn, his eyes filled with pain and emotional anguish.

'Phillips, sir, Sergeant Damien Phillips.' Damien grabbed Finn's gown, yanking him close, jarring his already throbbing upper arm and neck. 'Don't let me die. I don't want to die.'

Finn suddenly felt the weight of the promise he'd made to his brother all those years ago. It burned as fiercely on his conscience at this moment as it had that day sprawled in the dirt of a land far away. A promise he'd known, crippled by his own injuries and with help too many precious minutes away, he couldn't keep.

A promise that had haunted him.

But he could make good on a promise to Damien. In this top-notch facility and with his top-notch skills.

And he'd be damned if he'd lose another soldier on his watch.

'I won't, Damien. I won't.'

Evie looked at him sharply as a nurse passed her a chest tube. The soldier and Finn were practically nose to nose but, still, the husky promise surprised her. And not just because of the raw emotion she could hear in it.

Had Finn gone mad? Why on earth would he make such a promise? Damien's injuries were extensive—no one could promise that. Not even someone with Finn's legendary skill!

'Blood pressure ninety systolic.'

Finn glanced at her and she sucked in a breath at the brief flash of anguish, like the sweep of a lighthouse beacon, she saw there. His piercing gaze clouded temporarily with something she couldn't put her finger on—pain, compassion, loss?—then cleared as he stood abruptly.

'Let's get him prepped for Theatre,' Finn ordered.

Two hours later, in the thick of the operating theatre after Finn had demanded she scrub in, Evie's shoulders ached and her neck was stiff as they battled to plug the holes in Damien's heart. They'd replaced his entire circulation with donated blood products twice over. And he was still bleeding.

No one was surprised when a life-threatening arrhythmia caused a sudden dangerous dip in his blood pressure.

But Finn didn't give up.

He had the young soldier's heart in his two bloodied hands and was squeezing it as if he could make the heart start beating again through sheer force of will.

He'd promised.

Too much death. Too many young men like Damien. Like Isaac.

Damn it! He'd promised.

But as the downtime extended, even he could see the futility of it. Finn found it hard to breathe as he gently removed his hands from around the soldier's heart and stepped back. He peeled off his gloves and glanced at the clock.

'Time of death fifteen thirty-one.'

No one spoke as they watched Finn walk out of the theatre. But a little bit of Evie went with him.

An hour later after attending to all the legalities, Evie felt drained, totally strung out from the after-effects of adrenaline and their exhaustive yet futile efforts to save Sergeant Damien Phillips's life.

Except it wasn't over because she had to find Finn, who wasn't answering his page. He had to sign some paperwork.

And she was worried about him...

Her fingers trembled as she pushed the change-room doors open. She needed to get out of these scrubs. They reminded her too much of the tragedy she'd just witnessed.

Of Finn's hands squeezing Damien's dying heart.

Her heart leapt in her chest as Finn came into view. He was sitting on the floor, staring at the wall, the lockers supporting his back. His knees were bent up and his hands were hanging between them, his surgical cap dangling from his fingers.

She swallowed. 'I've been paging you.'

Finn heard her voice as if from far away. He didn't want her there. He didn't want her to look at him with those calm hazel eyes of hers, eyes that saw too much, and mouth some horrible cliché.

He wanted to go home, pour himself a Scotch. And then another one. Drink until he could be sure he wouldn't dream about Isaac.

He kept his gaze firmly fixed on the wall. 'I've been ignoring you.'

Evie stared at him, dismayed at the return of his churlish tone. She should have expected it but for some reason, after their frantic efforts with Damien and the shared horror of losing him, she'd thought it'd be different.

He'd be different.

Irritated, she sauntered over to the patch of wall he was fixated on and deliberately parked her butt on it. Now he had no choice but to look at her. She folded her arms.

'There's some paperwork for the coroner you need to sign out in the office.'

Finn flicked his gaze up to her determined face. 'Fine.'

They stared at each other for a moment, the blue of Finn's eyes even more pronounced against the blue of his scrubs. Evie battled the urge to debrief, as she would normally with a colleague who had shared such an emotionally intense situation. Even a churlish one. But everything about Finn said, *Back off.*

But, then, when hadn't it?

'Damien's been taken to the morgue and—'

Finn pushed himself to his feet, interrupting her words. He bit down on a wince as a hot needle jabbed viciously into the nerves that ran down his right arm.

'We're not talking about Damien,' he said, turning to his locker, his back deliberately to her.

Evie took in the expanse of his back in his scrubs as she reeled from the vehemence in his words.

But I want to talk about him. I had my hand in his chest too, felt his heart pulsating. I need to talk about him.

She pushed off the wall and took a tentative step towards him and even though she knew she was overstepping the line, she didn't seem to be able to stop.

'Finn.'

His back stayed stubbornly turned away. Evie stared at it and let out the breath she'd been holding. She waited for a moment and stepped closer. 'Maybe it'd help…to talk about it?' she murmured.

His silence was absolute and out of pure frustration she tentatively placed her hand on his left shoulder. Despite the flinch she felt right down to her soul, Mia kept it there. His muscles were knotted with tension, practically vibrating beneath her hand, and she moved closer again until her body was almost touching his.

Finn shut his eyes as her scent and her warmth enveloped him. He could sense her right there behind him. Could hear the soft huff of her breath and the empathy oozing from every pore. A part of him wanted to unburden so badly it was shocking in its intensity.

Would it hurt to lean back a little, to have just a moment today that made sense?

Even if it didn't?

Evie held her breath as his body swayed a little and then seemed to slowly relax back against hers. His scrubs felt warm on her skin and she could sense the vitality of him as they stood in silence, cradled against each other, her cheek brushing his shoulder blade.

It was a magical moment and she shut her eyes to absorb every second. Everything suddenly seemed… right. Evie felt safe. She felt understood.

'You were brilliant today,' he whispered.

Evie eyes fluttered open at the barely discernible words. Had he said it or had she only imagined it? She opened her mouth to return the compliment but a beeping pager shattered the intimacy.

Finn's eyes opened instantly. His surroundings came

into sharp focus, the feel of Evie pressed against him suddenly too, too close for comfort.

What the hell was he doing?

He shrugged her away. 'I have to go,' he said gruffly.

Evie stepped back from him, reeling from the quick severing of the fragile emotional connection they'd just made.

He didn't even look back as he departed.

Mia headed straight for Pete's Bar after work later that evening. It had been a harrowing day for all of them, with Evie seeming particularly stressed when she'd finally returned to the department. They'd arranged to meet for a drink and a bit of a debrief session. Her friend was obviously taking the soldier's death hard.

Evie, however, was nowhere to be seen amidst the surprising Sunday night crowd as Mia made her way to the bar.

Luca, on the other hand, was easily spotted by her specially tuned senses and even if she'd been able to resist his devilish smile, she couldn't resist his I've-been-waiting-for-you stare.

Luca slid over as Mia approached, a sense of inevitability taking hold. What was it about this woman that made him want more? Her complete lack of sexual inhibitions or was she just a novelty, something familiar for a change instead of just another pick-up?

Or maybe it was her emotional unavailability? Knowing that she wanted the same thing he did—no commitments, nothing but a good time.

He watched the tame swish of her ponytail as she came closer, knowing what that hair looked like loose and wild and knowing from the heat in her gaze that tonight was going to get very wild indeed.

Mia refused to look at Luca as she slid in beside him. She didn't want to alert the two other occupants to what was going on between them. She and Luca were sex—just sex—and she didn't want the others to get the wrong impression.

She greeted Charlie Maxwell, the orthopaedic surgeon who had operated on the partially severed leg earlier, and Carl Todd, the anaesthetist. They were chatting about the bomb blast at Douglas and the two operations that had followed.

'He's not out of the woods yet,' Charlie said, taking a mouthful of his cola. He was on call and could well be called back to amputate the leg. 'We managed to save it but I'm not entirely convinced it'll be viable in the long term. There was extensive blood loss and a lengthy ischaemic time.'

Mia was always surprised whenever Charlie was serious. The lovable, laid-back, ex-pro surfer with his shaved head and wicked sense of humour gave new meaning to the Aussie word 'larrikin'. It was hard to tell at first glance that beneath it all he was a dedicated and committed professional.

'The trip from the army barracks isn't exactly short,' Mia mused. They were the nearest tertiary hospital to the barracks but in a situation where every second was vital, it was just a little too far away.

'Absolutely,' Charlie agreed. 'You guys did a great job getting him to me as quickly as you could.'

They chatted about the procedure for a while and Mia was pleased to hear that the patient was still stable in ICU with good pulses when Charlie rang to get an update.

Working on saving the leg today with Luca had been an exhilarating experience, and it was good to know that their efforts had contributed to the thus far positive operative outcome.

She glanced at Luca and felt her breath hitch as he chose that moment to glance at her. Heat surged up the side seam of her jeans where their legs touched. Under the table, his hand slid onto her thigh.

She felt her breath seize in her lungs. But, as his fingers started to smooth the fabric of her jeans in light patterns, she didn't remove it.

'Well, at least you had better luck than Finn,' Carl commented, dragging Mia's attention back to the conversation. He inclined his head to indicate the man in question, who was sitting at the bar by himself, staring into his Scotch.

'He worked like a demon, trying to save the other soldier. It was like he was possessed or something.'

Even knowing how much Carl liked to embellish things, Mia was startled by the anaesthetist's description of the frantic efforts in Finn's theatre that afternoon—no wonder Evie needed to debrief.

'Evie's pretty wrecked,' Mia commented when Carl finished.

'She's in the wrong specialty. She'd make a great surgeon,' Carl mused. 'Kept her head no matter how testy Finn got.'

Mia glanced at Finn again just as Suzy plonked herself down in the chair next to him. The theatre nurse was a regular at Pete's and Mia had seen her flirting with Finn here before, but a blind fool could see that Finn was not in the mood for company.

He gave her one of those polite frozen smiles she'd seen Finn give once too often to hapless medical students or to Eric Frobisher in particular, but Suzy seemed as oblivious or impervious to Finn's signals as Eric did.

Luca's signals, however, as his fingers continued to brush against her thigh, were loud and clear. Mia fought the urge to turn her body towards him, raise her mouth to his.

Carl looked over his shoulder again. 'Well, well, well. Looks like Finn's found a little distraction for the night.'

Mia just stopped the eye-roll. Carl was a top-class anaesthetist and still fancied himself as a bit of a ladies' man but he obviously wasn't a student of body language—he was way off the mark.

Luca winked at her. 'Oh, you think so?' he asked, watching an obviously distant Finn.

Carl took a swallow of his beer. 'Oh, yes.' He tapped his nose three times with his index finger. 'I've been around long enough to tell when there's hanky-panky going on between the staff.'

Luca felt Mia's thigh tense beneath his palm and he grinned. 'Really?' he murmured as he resisted Mia's sudden attempt to remove his hand from her thigh.

He easily won the necessarily subdued struggle.

Carl nodded. 'Of course. I picked Luke and Lily long before anyone else did. And this bloke…' he jerked his thumb towards Charlie. '…is virtually an open book.'

Charlie looked affronted. 'Me? What about him?' Charlie pointed to Luca. 'His reputation *preceded* him.'

'Ah, well.' Carl laughed. 'That's true.'

Luca laughed good-naturedly. 'And what about Mia?'

he enquired innocently, daring to stroke his fingers closer to the apex of her thighs. He didn't even wince when his ankle suffered a short, sharp jab from a hard pointy toe. 'Any gossip on her?'

Carl shook his head with a faux crestfallen look. 'Oh, no. Mia informed me a long time ago that fooling around with someone from work was a recipe for disaster. I think they were the words, right, Mia?'

Mia nodded her head graciously. She'd told Carl that most emphatically one day just after he'd tried to come on to her. And she meant it as much now as she had then.

So why the hell was she sitting at a booth with an Italian devil who was practically bringing her to orgasm in front of two oblivious colleagues?

Surely Carl could see the pheromones wafting off her body?

'What?' Luca feigned shock, looking down into Mia's face, gratified to see heat shimmering in her eyes like a mirage as his finger found her inner seam. He noticed her knuckles whiten as her grip on the edge of the table tightened. 'There's been no work flirtations?'

'Oh, no,' Carl answered for her. 'As far as I can tell, there's been no one. And I have a pretty good radar,' he added, tapping his nose again and smiling at Mia.

Luca flicked a finger across the seam that ran down from the bottom of her zip where it joined the two inner thigh seams. He felt her resistance melt to nothing as her legs eased apart a little and he thought, *Carl, you are a fool!*

Mia knew she shouldn't. They were in a public place, for crying out loud. A place that was crawling with staff from The Harbour. But his fingers were creating such delicious havoc…and no one could see…

She spread her legs a little further and smiled at Charlie as she changed the subject.

Evie was late to Pete's but that was the nature of the job. A last-minute patient had kept her involved for a while, which had been fine by her. Becoming absorbed in her work had helped keep her mind off Finn and what had happened between them today.

Because, whether he liked it or not—whether *she* liked it or not—something *had* happened. She'd had a glimpse of his humanity and no matter how many patients she'd seen since, she just couldn't banish that from her head.

And that brief moment when he'd leaned into her… It had felt like some kind of…surrender.

She'd never seen Finn emotionally vulnerable but today had been different. Today he'd leaned on her. Actually let himself go for once and trusted her enough to drop the cantankerous-but-brilliant-surgeon facade and just be a doctor who'd lost a patient. Be human. Be a man.

She could still feel the imprint of him against her. The flat of his shoulder blade against her cheek, the warm, solid roundness of his shoulder beneath her palm, the press of his broad back against her chest, their hearts beating almost as one.

She wasn't stupid enough to read anything into it. But she was intrigued. She wanted to know more. She wanted to know what had happened in his past to make Damien's case so personal to Finn. So personal that he'd let his guard down to her, of all people. Let her touch him. Let himself touch her back.

You were brilliant today, Evie.

Those words had meant more to her than any compliment she'd ever received-professional or personal. She hugged them to herself as she crossed the road to Pete's.

If Finn was at Pete's, she was going to repay the compliment. She was going to buy him a drink, tell him he was brilliant and badger him until he talked.

Staff at The Harbour always talked about what a maverick he was, what a legend. They held him in awe, hoisted him on high like some kind of trophy, made him untouchable. Like he was a machine, a robot. But they seemed to forget, underneath it all he was also a man.

But she hadn't. She'd seen the man today.

And men needed to be touched too.

Finn probably most of all.

Finn wasn't really listening to Suzy as she prattled on about some movie she'd just seen. He didn't want her there, he didn't want to talk or make light conversation.

He didn't want to hook up. Even if Suzy was extremely attractive and obviously up for it.

He came to Pete's for one reason only. To drink.

Sure, he could drink at home. And he'd do that too. But drinking a little in public tempered the urge to drink a lot when he got back to his apartment.

The Scotch helped with the pain from his injuries and it helped obliterate the events that had caused them.

Suzy couldn't do that. No woman could. Not even Lydia.

And then Evie's lovely face entered his vision and

for one crazy moment panic rose in him as he thought he'd conjured her up. But then she pushed the heavy door open wider and their gazes met.

For a moment there was a shimmer of recognition between them, a whisper of what they'd both endured together, and then she smiled at him, a smile that seemed to see right inside him. A smile that said, I know you're hurting; let me help you.

And for one mad instant he wanted that. He wanted to feel again what he'd felt that afternoon in the change room cocooned against her. That strange kind of peace—like nothing he'd ever known.

The panic intensified.

The sheer power of these strange, unwanted feelings Evie evoked overwhelmed him. He dragged his gaze away, his heart beating like that of a wild animal suddenly caged and fighting for his life. She didn't know him. She didn't know anything about him. How could she? Princess Evie couldn't even begin to comprehend where he'd come from, the things he'd seen, the promises he'd broken.

He turned to Suzy and dazzled her with a smile. 'Whaddya say we get out of here?'

Evie, her heart light as she spotted Finn, made a direct line for him. She stopped three paces later when she realised he wasn't alone. The smile he gave the blonde, one she'd seen him with here before, took her breath away and she struggled with the sudden urge to turn on her heel and run.

Or slap someone. *Back off!*

But he wasn't hers to make such an order. The realisation brought with it a sudden crushing sense of despair. Just because they'd shared a moment, that didn't make him hers.

Finn smiled down at Suzy as she leaned forward and whispered in his ear. Her cleavage was exposed to his view and he looked his fill.

It was an impressive cleavage and he was a man, damn it.

A man who appreciated a woman's body but did *not* get emotionally involved with them. And the sooner Evie got that through her head, the better.

He wasn't some wounded hero that needed saving. He was a cantankerous bastard beyond redemption.

'C'mon,' he said, sliding off the stool, putting his hand out to help Suzy off hers but looking directly over her head, meeting Evie's shocked look with practised indifference. 'Let's go back to my place.'

Evie couldn't move for a moment, the cold of Finn's piercing gaze freezing her to the spot. He seemed totally unreachable as his eyes told her things he couldn't say in a crowded bar.

Like*, what happened this afternoon meant nothing. You mean nothing.*

Suzy smiled up at Finn, disconcerted to find he wasn't looking at her. 'I thought you'd never ask.'

Finn dragged his gaze away from the emotions in Evie's hazel eyes. There was hurt and disgust and even a touch of scorn.

And he deserved every one of them.

He threw another dazzler Suzy's way before tucking her hand in his, straightening his back and making a beeline for the door.

Evie watched him go, a veritable storm of emotions raging inside. Anger, repulsion, despair.

Where was the Finn from earlier? The one who had leaned into her and told her she was brilliant?

She looked back to find Pete watching her. He was holding up a cold beer and a shot glass and his gaze radiated warmth and sympathy.

Thank God for Pete.

CHAPTER SEVEN

TWENTY minutes later Charlie drained his glass and stood. 'I'm going to go and check on my patient.'

'That's very dedicated of you,' Mia teased, wishing both he and Carl would leave so she could drag Luca into the nearest dark corner and have him finish what he started, instead of taunting her in secret with those very clever fingers.

But she'd soon learned that two could play at his game and Luca was looking decidedly uncomfortable himself.

'Of course the delectable Nurse Barry has nothing to do with it,' Carl added.

Charlie grinned. 'I'm affronted, Carl.' And grinned again.

Carl tossed back his beer. 'Hang on, then, I'll walk you out.'

They said their goodbyes and Luca and Mia were finally left alone. Luca dropped his mouth to her ear. 'You're going to pay for that. Let's go. Now.'

Mia smiled as his voice, thick with lust, emphasised his accent. A surge of anticipation tightened her pelvic floor. 'If you can't take it,' she murmured, sliding slowly out of the booth, 'you shouldn't be dishing it out.'

'Here you are, Mia. Sorry I'm late,' Evie said, plonking herself down on the opposite seat, pushing a tray of orange juice, beer and shot glasses onto the table. 'I'm warning you now, I plan on getting very, very drunk.'

Mia shut her eyes briefly. *Damn. Evie.*

Luca's caress had managed to erase all trace of the reason she'd come to Pete's tonight in the first place. She glanced at Luca, saw lust rippling through the dark chocolate pools of his eyes and felt everything clench. She forced herself to look away.

'I can see that,' Mia murmured, as Evie raised the shot glass to her lips.

'Oh, hello, Luca,' Evie said as she slammed down the first shot and lined up her second. 'So glad you're here. Maybe you can explain to me how the male mind works?'

Luca looked from Mia to Evie and back to Mia again. He'd had a vision of how the evening was going to pan out and this had not been part of it. He watched as Evie threw back her second shot and knew enough about women to know that he had one too many y chromosomes to be a part of this conversation.

He glanced at Mia, who shrugged an apology at him, a small smile playing on her lips. He stroked up the centre seam of her jeans and was gratified to see the smile disappear.

He patted her leg twice. 'I think I'll go and leave you lovely ladies to it.'

Mia scooted out and Luca followed her, her rear end at an enticing level before he stood and towered over her.

He nodded at Evie. 'Goodnight.'

Evie grunted something as she contemplated her

third shot and he turned to Mia. 'I'll see you...' he quirked an eyebrow at her '...soon?'

Mia watched as Evie downed another tequila. 'Later.' She grimaced.

Luca dropped his gaze to her mouth then sighed. 'Later.'

It was low and raw and whispered along her nerve endings and Mia felt decidedly wobbly as she slid back into the booth, her insides melting.

'Are you okay?' she asked Evie, refusing to turn and watch Luca walk out of the bar. Pete had already given her a speculative look as she'd sat—she didn't want anyone else in the bar wising up.

Evie shook her head. 'Nope. But I will be.' She slammed another shot back. 'Real soon.'

Mia sipped her orange juice. 'You won't be in the morning.'

'Well, I have two days until I'm back on shift to re-cover.'

Mia pushed the beer towards her friend and dragged the tray with three more shots on it out of reach. 'You may well need them.'

Evie didn't protest, just sipped at her beer.

'Carl was telling me you had a pretty harrowing time in Theatre with Finn. Tell me about it.'

Evie raised her eyes to her best friend. 'Oh, Mia, it was the most incredible thing I've ever witnessed. Finn was...he was...magnificent.' She sipped her beer again. 'And then he went and acted like a total jerk.'

Mia nodded. 'Okay, start at the beginning.'

Three hours later Evie had unburdened and Mia had managed to stagger home with her and put her to bed.

She left a jug of water, a glass and two tablets by Evie's bed for when she woke up feeling like someone was drilling for oil in her brain, her mouth as dry and putrid as the newspaper that lined a budgie cage.

She watched her friend sleep for a moment. Evie really had it bad. She didn't know it yet, of course, but a man who drove a girl that crazy was more than some nutty crush.

Which was why her way was much better. Give them your body but keep your heart and mind out of contention. Use them for sex then walk away.

Like her and Luca.

Except she hadn't walked away, had she?

She looked at Evie's face, troubled even in an alcohol-induced slumber. If this was what pining after a man got you then she wanted no part of it.

She had to end it with Luca.

After tonight.

Mia glanced at Evie's bedside clock—it was nearly one in the morning. Would Luca be awake?

She remembered how hard he'd been beneath his jeans as she'd fondled him under the table.

He'd be awake.

Her own body was still humming like an electrical substation generating enough heat to power the entire eastern seaboard.

She smiled to herself as she hurried to her bedroom, stripping off her clothes, pulling her hair out of its ponytail, opening her wardrobe, yanking her long winter coat off its hanger and stepping into its folds, the lining cool against her bare, heated flesh. She overlapped the edges and tied the cord securely around her waist—

there were buttons but they were going to take too long to undo for her purposes.

Mia inspected herself in the mirror. She looked very modest in the calf-length coat and heels. Should she, on the slim off chance at after one in the morning, happen to bump into someone in the lift, they couldn't possibly be aware she didn't have a stitch on under the coat.

Neither would Luca.

Mia smiled at her reflection. All she needed was a little eye make-up and some lippy and she'd be perfect for an early-morning booty call.

Hell, if this was going to be their last time, she might as well blow his mind.

Luca was brooding in front of his magnificent bay window when he heard the knock. He allowed himself a smile for the first time since arriving home alone with a raging hard-on over three hours ago.

Anticipation tightened his groin as he stalked to the door and yanked it open to find a rugged up Mia leaning casually against the jamb.

'Oh, good.' She smiled. 'You're awake.'

Luca sucked in a breath. Her hair was loose and her eyes were heavily kohled in shades of grey and black, emphasising their blueness. Her mouth was painted fire-engine red. He moved in close until their bodies were almost touching. 'It's hard to sleep in my condition,' he murmured.

Mia pouted. 'Poor darling. Can I come in? I could help you with that.'

Luca's gaze drifted to her mouth. 'Are you sure? I wouldn't want you entering into a recipe for disaster.'

Mia laughed as devilish memories from Pete's surfaced. Luca touching her under the table, stroking between her legs. She lifted a finger and traced his bottom lip, almost moaning out loud when he sucked it into his mouth. 'Carl's a sore loser,' she whispered.

Luca, his body taut with longing, swirled his tongue around her finger and gently released it. 'Come in, take your clothes off. You are way overdressed.'

He stepped back and Mia strode into the room. The heat enveloped her and she turned to find Luca watching her from the shut door. She untied the coat and shrugged out of it. It fell to the floor and she was standing before him in nothing but a pair of heels.

'Will this do?' she asked.

Luca's brain temporarily powered down as his hungry gaze ate up her body. Her long legs, the jut of her breasts, the flare of her hips, the shadow of her sex.

Mia's nipples hardened at the intensity of his scrutiny. It felt more intimate than if he'd touched her and she suddenly felt like he could see right inside her. She fought the urge to cover herself.

Luca swallowed. 'Spin around.'

His husky command spread tentacles of heat through her belly and she performed a slow teasing rotation, looking over her shoulder at him as she circled her hips like she'd seen once in a documentary on pole dancing.

Luca's belly clenched tight. He pushed away from the door and was in front of her, reaching for her in seconds, his hands sliding around her waist, his mouth descending.

And then he was kissing her and she was kissing him back. Long, deep, wet kisses that had her gasping and sighing and begging for more as she pulled at his clothes, desperate for some skin on skin.

Her nipples rubbed against his naked chest and Luca groaned deep in his throat. Then he swept her up into his arms and strode through the apartment, their mouths locked, their hearts beating to a rhythm that pulsed like a rock concert through the air around them.

Luca reached his bed and threw her on it. Mia was startled as she free-fell, landing softly but breathing hard. Somewhere along the way she'd lost her heels so she was one hundred per cent naked now.

She looked up at a half-undressed Luca. His lips were moist from their kissing, his shirt was half off, his zipper undone.

'You look good,' she murmured.

Luca grinned. 'You look better.'

Then he was stripping off his clothes, reaching for a condom, sheathing himself, then joining her, tangling his limbs with hers, kissing her mouth and her neck and her breasts, ignoring her entreaties to finish it as he licked lower. And lower.

It wasn't until she lay spent beneath him that he succumbed to his own body's dictates, entering her slowly, revelling in her exultant cry, rocking and pulsing, building her again until he was pounding and pounding, pushing them both to impossible heights and then pushing them both over into oblivion.

It was several minutes before either of them was physically able to speak. Luca, who was now lying on his back, recovered first.

'Do you realise this is the first time we've actually done it in a bed?'

Mia, her brain cells still reorganising themselves after a mass meltdown, just nodded. It took her another couple of minutes to process and for a spike of worry to register.

Somehow landing in Luca's bed made this whole thing seem more intimate. The other places had personified their relationship—the on-call room, the shower, the kitchen bench. Quick and impersonal.

Places to get off then move on.

They had spelled temporary, fleeting, momentary.

But to be in his bed, in his bedroom? What the hell did that spell?

Mia didn't think it was prudent to stick around and find out. Just as soon as she could move without her legs collapsing, she was out of here. The perfect opportunity arose when Luca went to the bathroom to relieve himself of the condom but her legs refused to co-operate so she was still lying stark naked on his bed when he returned.

'You look good there,' Luca murmured as he approached the bed.

Mia watched him draw nearer, unashamedly naked, his beautiful smooth face and body a sight to behold. Desire stirred in her belly.

Right, that was it! *Get up now, McKenzie!*

Except the phone beside Luca's bed chose that moment to ring, scaring the living daylights out of her. She glanced at the clock. 'Who on earth is ringing at this ungodly hour?'

Luca felt his heart rate accelerate. *People who lived in places where it wasn't an ungodly hour.*

He reached the phone in three purposeful strides and snatched it up. *'Ciao.'*

Mia saw another chance to escape but Luca talking in his native tongue was such a treat, even if she didn't understand a word, she just lay and listened to him. He sat on the side of the bed his back to her, and she resisted the urge to run her palm up and down the broad expanse of his ribs. To contrast the white of her skin with the tantalising copper of his.

The first sign that the phone call wasn't social was Luca raising his voice. He raked his hand through his hair and seemed to be demanding something of the caller. She heard the word '*nonna*' a lot. Wasn't that Italian for grandmother? Had something happened to his grandmother?

There was some more rapid-fire conversation before Luca hung up, tossing the hands-free receiver onto the bedside table with a clatter.

Mia pushed herself up on to her elbows, staring at the solid wall of his back. 'Is everything okay?' she asked tentatively.

Luca dragged himself back from the brink of the abyss the phone call had taken him to. For a moment he'd forgotten Mia was even there. He was inordinately pleased she was.

Which didn't sit well at all.

He rubbed the back of his neck. 'No. That was a cousin of mine. My grandmother is dead.'

Mia heard the husky rawness behind the blunt delivery and in that instant she forgot that she was naked, forgot that she was supposed to have already gone, forgot that she didn't get involved. The driving need to offer him comfort, as she would do anyone—a friend, a patient a colleague—overrode everything.

She sat and scooted over to him shunting in behind him, spreading her legs to accommodate him, his bottom fitting snugly into the cradle of her pelvis, her thighs bracketing his.

She leaned her torso into him, her breasts squashed against his back. Her hands found his arms, her palms running up and down the warm solid weight of his biceps.

'I'm sorry,' she murmured, her cheek resting against his shoulder blade. 'Were you close?'

Luca nodded. Regret, never far away, twisted the ever-present knife deep into his heart. He had been the apple of his nonna's eye. Even after that horrible day that had changed his family life for ever.

She'd been the only one who'd believed there was more to Luca than the irresponsible teenager who had let everyone down.

Turning his back on her had been a particular wrench.

'We spoke once a week.' It was how he knew his family still hadn't forgiven him.

Mia absently brushed her mouth against Luca's back once, twice, three times. His muscles seemed to be quivering beneath her lips and she knew she couldn't leave him like this.

'It's okay, Luca,' she murmured. 'C'mon, lie down for a while.'

She scooted back, until she was sitting propped up a little against the bedhead, and placed a hand on his shoulder. For a moment she thought he was going to resist but then he let her pull him down so the back of his head was cradled against her shoulder, her arm braced across his chest.

Luca lay still as Mia settled the sheet in around them. He turned his face and nuzzled her arm, inhaling her fragrance, letting the beat of her heart close to his ear soothe the ache in his chest.

'Do you want to talk about her?' she asked, trailing the fingers of her free hand up and down his arm.

Luca shook his head. He didn't want to talk, he didn't want to think. He just wanted to lie here next to her and forget the world.

'Okay. We'll just lie here for a bit, then.'

So they did.

She had absolutely no intention of staying. Absolutely no intention of falling asleep. No intention whatsoever other than to offer a little bit of comfort and companionship in Luca's time of need.

She really, really didn't mean to fall asleep.

Or stay the night…

Mia woke to the most delicious feeling of warmth. Of being wrapped in a cocoon of contentment. She stretched languorously against all that solid heat behind her then snuggled back into it again. A heaviness at her hip spanned her waist and curled around her breast. A delicious sensation buzzed her neck. A hardness nudged at the cleft of her bottom.

Hmm. Luca.

She sighed as sleep wrapped her in a sticky embrace. For five seconds.

Then panic set in.

Luca!

Damn! What time was it?

She cracked open one eye, then the other, squinting at the digital clock on the bedside table. Eight-fifteen.

In the morning.

Damn, damn, triple damn!

She lay very still for a long moment, listening to him breathe, not daring to do so herself. It was deep and even. Was he asleep? His lips had brushed her neck only seconds ago but had that been involuntary?

His hand at her breast, tantalising and erotic, seemed lax. Not that her nipple seemed to know the difference as it scrunched and scraped erotically against the flat of his palm.

Neither, for that matter, did his erection. She could feel it nestled against her, big and heavy.

Ready for action.

How the hell could he sleep with that thing? Surely his brain was being deprived of oxygen?

Mia waited a bit longer for signs of life. Other than his erection.

No. He was definitely asleep.

She took that as her cue to get the hell out. What had she been thinking? She didn't do this. She didn't stay the night. She didn't…spoon.

Hell, she didn't even cuddle.

And he knew that!

Okay, no one she'd ever been to bed with had received a phone call that their grandmother had died either—but that was beside the point. She was supposed to have left hours ago. She couldn't let one man's personal life alter years of self-discipline.

She'd very nearly failed medical school, thrown away her future, by letting men and booze rule her life for those couple of crazy years after she'd found out about her father, about her mother's deception. She'd made a promise to herself back then that it would never happen again.

And Luca was no exception.

Yes, he'd transcended her staunch one-night-stand policy. But he was still just a convenient body—hot, sexy, best she'd-ever-known body—and that was all.

Dead grandmother or not.

Her decision from last night—before she'd totally messed up and stayed—to end things with Luca suddenly just got a whole lot more urgent.

Mia didn't breathe again until she'd slunk very carefully out of his bed and tiptoed out of his room. Thankfully the central heating was still on because it looked like a frosty old day through those big bay windows as a stiff breeze blew across the harbour, rippling the surface like goose-bumps on flesh.

She strode to the centre of the room and scooped up her jacket, shrugging into it, again ignoring the buttons as she tied it at the waist.

Now, where the hell were her shoes?

She quickly scanned the shoeless route from the lounge to Luca's bedroom. Her gaze stopped at his doorway.

Please, don't make me go back there.

She didn't need the temptation of a sleeping Luca. She hadn't looked back as she'd fled the room and she didn't want to know now either. She needed to get out.

She'd leave her bloody shoes if she had to. Even if her feet would be half-frozen by the time she reached her apartment.

Yes, she needed to tell him this wouldn't be happening again. Especially now. Especially after last night.

But she could leave that for tomorrow. For now she needed to get out. And quickly.

Her panicked gaze backtracked, sweeping a broader area than before. It snagged on a partially obscured heel somehow under the bar stools that lined the central kitchen bench.

Wow. She must have kicked them off wildly—or had Luca pulled them off then tossed them across the room?

Her mind had been mush at the time.

Mia quickly retrieved it, trying not to think about just what she and Luca had done on that kitchen bench. How he'd swept aside the dirty dishes and taken her right there on the cold granite bench top.

Stop it! Don't go there!

Mia shook herself. One shoe down, one to go. She refined her search—if one had ended up near the kitchen, the other one could be anywhere. She dropped to her knees in front of the lounge suite and looked under the chairs.

Bingo!

She reached under for it but the lounge didn't have a lot of clearance and she had to get down lower to even get her fingers to it. She extended her arm further and finally dragged it out, giving a triumphant murmur as she sat back on her haunches.

'What are you doing?'

Mia lurched abruptly to her feet. Luca was leaning against the doorframe, in nothing but underpants, his arms crossed, a small frown making a harsh line out of his beautiful mouth. There was a shadow in his eyes that was a perfect foil for the one darkening his jaw and seemed to match his serious countenance.

'Luca.' Mia, excruciatingly aware of her nakedness beneath the coat, absently kicked first one foot up behind her and then the other as she slid the shoes in place, 'Sorry…couldn't find my shoes.'

Luca watched as she shimmied into her stilettos.

Usually he liked the way women did that. It was sexy. But this morning the death of his grandmother and the burden of guilt he felt over his absence in her life weighed heavily.

As did Mia being witness to it all.

This morning he was immune to sexy.

When he'd woken alone he'd been relieved. His vulnerability last night had shaken him. He wasn't used to being that emotionally exposed to anyone, least of all a woman. Marissa had burned him for life in that regard and he had no desire to repeat the experience.

The last thing he needed this morning was to see pity in Mia's eyes.

He needed to be alone.

'I need coffee,' he said abruptly, pushing away from the doorframe.

Mia watched him stride to the kitchen, a very different man from the post-coital Luca she'd come to know. No sexy smile, no lazy laugh, no knowing gaze. And certainly very different from the man she'd held last night, who'd fallen asleep in her arms.

He seemed to have erected a wall and was putting her firmly on the outside.

Which was great. *Exactly what she wanted.* Exactly what she'd been hoping for. No need for the big talk after all. Just slip out of his apartment and consider it over.

Perfect.

If only her body wasn't rebelling. The site of his strong, naked back, the way the muscles played beneath the fine moulding of copper flesh, the sexy indentation of the small of his back was causing a riot amongst her hormones. She ground her feet into the carpet to stop herself taking a step towards him.

When had her body started to crave his like this? It was so…base.

'I'm going to go,' she announced to his back. 'Check that Evie hasn't slipped into an alcoholic coma. And you have a lot to organise today.'

Luca frowned as he filled the percolator with water. 'Organise?'

'Flights, time off work, packing.'

'Flights?'

It was Mia's turn to frown. 'For the funeral? I'm sorry, I assumed your grandmother lived in Italy? Is she here in Sydney?'

He hadn't told her that. But, then, why would he? They didn't…chat. They'd had sex a few times. That's what they did. That's all they did.

Until last night.

And it was why they were over now. Now that their relationship had evolved to a level of emotional intimacy neither of them wanted.

Luca flipped the switch on the coffee machine and turned to face her, his hands gripping the bench behind him, his knuckles white. 'I'm not going to the funeral.'

Mia blinked. 'What?'

'I'm not going,' he repeated.

'But…I thought you said you were close to your grandmother?'

Her yearning for a grandmother of her own, someone who could have softened the harsh realities of her childhood, been a buffer even, returned as Mia struggled to understand what Luca was saying.

Luca nodded. 'I am.' He raked a hand through his

hair as he realised what he'd said. 'I was… I haven't been back to Italy since the day I left and, trust me, no one in my family wants me to return.'

The edge of bitterness in his voice surprised Mia and instead of turning and walking to the door, which would have been the wisest course of action, she wandered closer to the kitchen.

'No one?'

He nodded grimly. 'Sicilians have long memories.'

Mia slid onto one of the stools, the urge to comfort him as strong as it had been last night despite his *keep-out* expression. 'Look, I don't know what happened with you and your family—'

She held up a hand as he opened his mouth to interrupt. He looked like he was going to tell her to mind her own damn business, which was fine by her. Apart from knowing he'd left Marsala at the age of sixteen, he hadn't told her about his past or the fact that he'd never been back.

And she didn't want to know. That wasn't what they were about—it was nothing to do with her.

Except she understood. She understood how things could be so bad that you'd never go back. How many times had she visited her mother in the last five years? Half a dozen? And how long ago had she given up on trying to keep in contact with a father who had moved on to a new family after the woman he'd loved had totally destroyed his old one?

'I don't want to know, Luca, but it was a long time ago, yeah? Maybe things are better now?'

Out of habit or manners, Luca poured two coffees and pushed one towards her. Even though he didn't want her to stay. He could see empathy in her gaze and wanted no part of it. They were just about sex—nothing else. Sex was all he did. He'd lost his head for a little while, but not any more.

'They're not.'

Mia stared down into the thick dark coffee—the colour of Luca's eyes. 'I'm sorry,' she murmured.

He shrugged. 'It's the way it is.'

Mia looked up sharply. She could see regret in his espresso gaze and hear a slight rawness to his accent. And suddenly she was mad. *Damn it!* Why was it that way? Why was he still being made to suffer twenty odd years later—this was his family. What had he done that had been so bad? Why did she feel guilty about not keeping her family together, about not keeping in contact when neither of her parents bothered? Why should she give a damn when they didn't?

'You should go,' she said.

Luca saw something glittering in her stained-glass-window eyes. They shone with an intense brightness that for a second looked almost like tears. But then it crystallised into determination.

He shook his head. 'Some things are better left alone, Mia.'

Mia shook her head emphatically. 'No, damn it! She was your grandmother and you loved her. And you need to go to her funeral and to hell with what everyone else thinks. You need this for you, Luca. You deserve this. Don't let them take this from you because of some stupid ancient history.'

Luca wasn't entirely sure that this passion was all about him and his predicament but he appreciated the sentiment. It was surprisingly good to have someone on his side in this whole family mess, even though she had no clue of the facts.

Another spurt of guilt made him uneasy. Would she be this passionate about it if she knew the background? Was she only being this vehement because she thought she knew him well enough to surmise that he'd been wronged by his family?

'Don't think I'm the injured party here, *cara*. They had every right to ostracise me. To be angry with me.'

His voice sounded far away in another time and Mia paused. She hadn't expected any explanation but she had expected him to defend himself when offering one. They'd ostracised him and he just accepted it?

'Still?' she demanded, regrouping. 'After all these years? Doesn't that make you angry?'

Luca shook his head. He'd given up being angry about it a long time ago. Regret was a constant companion—if he could go back and change things he would—but he'd worked through his anger.

'No. Not any more,' he said.

Mia couldn't believe how calm he was. She could feel a burning in her chest at his ostracism and hers. Her father leaving physically and her mother leaving emotionally had completely excluded her from the possibility of a normal life.

How could people who supposedly loved you act so callously? Even in grief? Her heart pounded, there was a ringing in her ears, her hands shook as she clasped them around the coffee cup.

It would be so easy to lose it. Just lose it. She hadn't been this stirred up in years. Maybe not since the day she'd discovered her stillborn baby sister hadn't been her father's child and that's why he'd left. That her mother had been lying to her for years.

She had a sudden insane urge to cry, which both scared and horrified her in equal measure. What the hell was wrong with her?

Mia McKenzie did not cry. Not in front of friends or colleagues and most certainly not lovers.

Not ever!

Luca was a man she'd had sex with a few times and slept with once. She shouldn't care about any of this.

She pulled herself back from the edge. Just. 'Well, I think you're wrong, but...' she shrugged with as much nonchalance as she could muster when her brain was melting down '...it's none of my business.'

She stood. She had to get out of there. The intensity of her feelings was scaring the hell out of her. He plainly didn't want her hanging around and she'd been trying to leave since the moment she'd woken with his hand on her breast.

Luca nodded, gripping the bench harder as the foolish urge to reach for her took hold. To put a hand on her shoulder, tug her into his arms. She looked a little wan and frankly he'd rather spend the day putting some colour back into her cheeks than thinking about his grandmother and the mess he'd left behind in Sicily.

But she'd turned away and was walking rapidly towards the door. Do not pass Go. Do not collect two hundred dollars.

'*Ciao*, Mia,' he called out.

Mia heard the finality in his voice and knew it was goodbye.

CHAPTER EIGHT

EVIE woke at ten-thirty feeling as if the New Year's Eve fireworks, for which Sydney was famous, had been let off in her head. All at once. She groaned out loud and stuffed the pillow over her head to quell the racket.

Not that it helped, given that the noise was coming from inside her skull, not from the outside.

The previous momentous day with Finn and then the bitter disappointment of the night came back in a rush and she groaned again. *Damn the man to hell.* It was his fault she felt this way.

She could only hope he'd been blessed with a hang-over of equal proportion. But, of course, he wouldn't have. Because the man could drink whisky like water. And because little Miss Suzy Happy Ending had been draped all over him when he'd left.

She didn't even want to think about why that bugged her so much. The man could sleep with whomever he liked. And quite often did. In the years they'd co-existed at The Harbour, he'd slept with a string of women.

It was no skin off her nose.

Just because Stuart's devastating betrayal had made her more selective with men, it didn't mean the entire world had to follow suit. If Finn wanted to sleep with every floozy Suzy that came along, more power to him.

Evie pulled the pillow off her head—damn it, now he'd made her think of Stuart. She'd been such a fool for that man, believing that he'd loved her when he'd been using her all along for her family connections.

She'd been humiliated and heartbroken and had endured the rather cruel twist of fate that had seen the hospital rumour mill peg her as the bitch of the piece. Apparently Dr Evie Lockheart had considered herself too good for the lowly Stuart.

It had taken her a long time to win back people's respect after that.

She was damned if she was going to lose that hard-won respect by making a fool of herself over another doctor. Especially one as arrogant and infuriating as Finn Kennedy.

The apartment was quiet when she entered the open-plan living area, pulling on a thick woolly dressing gown over the clothes she'd worn all day yesterday and apparently to bed too. She had a vague memory of Mia getting her home and helping her into bed but she must have drawn the line at undressing her.

She flicked on the jug and waited impatiently for it whistle. The aroma of coffee infused her senses as the boiling water hit the granules and Evie's stomach grumbled. She opened the fridge to grab the milk, only to find there was none.

Her stomach revolted. The fireworks in her head popped louder.

Oh, hell—she couldn't do black coffee. She just couldn't.

Without giving any thought to her appearance, she

shrugged out of her gown, grabbed a mug, pushed her feet into some discarded shoes by the door and was standing outside the lift in under thirty seconds.

Susie and John were bound to have milk.

Finally the lift arrived on her floor and for a second Evie almost wept. It was a short-lived emotion as the doors opened to reveal Suzy, also in the same clothes as last night, looking like she hadn't slept a wink. And not in that horrible bed-hair, bleary-eyed way that Evie was sporting. Oh, no. In that loose, relaxed, I've-had-all-my-kinks-ironed-out way.

Suzy smiled a bright, peppy smile. 'Hi, Dr Lockheart,' she chirped.

Evie cracked a small smile and gave what she hoped was a gracious nod because the alternative—launching herself at young, peppy, cute Suzy—was just not physically possible with a headache the size of Sydney Harbour.

Finn stared at the ceiling, absently massaging his right thumb to relieve the painful tingling, and wished he felt better after a very pleasant night with a gorgeous athletic young woman. But he didn't. And it had nothing to do with his physical injuries.

He kept seeing the look in Evie's eyes at Pete's last night. Those twin hazel pools had been like a damn open book as she'd telescoped her disapproval. The disgust and scorn he'd seen there he could live with. He saw them in the mirror every morning and he was pretty immune to them by now.

The hurt had been a lot harder to get past.

It reminded him a lot of Lydia and those horrible few years. Trying to make things better for her—easier—but only making them worse. His brother's widow had turned to him in a dark moment of grief and it had begun a long-drawn-out, complicated affair that he'd needed yet resented all at the same time.

Lydia had needed something that he hadn't been able to give—comfort. After a childhood in institutions and the horror of losing his brother, Finn just hadn't been capable of it. He hadn't known how to comfort himself let alone a grief-stricken widow.

It had been a relief when she'd finally moved on enough to end it. And yet, strangely, he'd also felt bereft. His one link to his little brother, the little brother he'd defended and protected from one care home to the next, the only constant in his childhood, had no longer been there.

The fact that he hadn't loved Lydia, or she him, hadn't mattered so much after she'd walked away.

So he knew exactly how a woman looked when she was hurt. And there'd been no doubt about it—Dr Evie Lockheart had been hurt last night. And he'd been responsible.

But, damn it all, could he help it if she'd read too much into a fleeting moment?

A temporary weakness?

Princess Evie could keep her goo-goo eyes to herself. He was fine. *Just fine.*

Mia was shocked to see Luca standing on her doorstep later that night. Between her morning-after regrets and Evie's monster hangover the day had dragged more slowly and become more depressing than a wet week.

She had been in her pyjamas and ready for bed when the knock had sounded. The cold air from the hallway rushed around her and she pulled her hot-pink polar fleece dressing gown closer.

'Luca?'

'Who is it?' Evie called from the couch, where she'd been watching old sitcom reruns all day.

'It's just Luca,' Mia threw over her shoulder as casually as she could. Because it could never be *just* Luca. The man was dressed in a suit and looked like a matinee idol, even with his face set grimly.

She really, really shouldn't want to drag him to her bedroom. But, heaven help her, she did.

Evie, her face fixed on the screen, laughed. 'Does he want to borrow a cup of milk?' And she laughed again.

Luca frowned. 'Huh?'

Mia shook her head. 'Long story.' She noticed a suitcase standing nearby in the hall. She raised an eyebrow. 'Going somewhere?'

He nodded. 'I decided to follow your advice.'

'You're going back to Italy?'

'Yes.' He gave her a ghost of a smile. 'To hell with them, right?'

Mia searched his face for a moment, pleased that he was doing the right thing but puzzled as to why he'd bothered to stop by and tell her.

The man was about to fly halfway around the world to go to his beloved grandmother's funeral against the wishes of a family he wasn't on good terms with and hadn't seen in over two decades—he probably didn't need her questions.

'Right,' she said awkwardly.

'I'll be back in five days,' he said.

'Five days? Hell, Luca, you're going to be next to useless when you return.' She saw something flit through his eyes and quickly added, 'Professionally,' in case he thought she'd meant it any other way.

She had no doubt that his *other* functions would be in *fine* working order.

Not that she cared or would be thinking about his other functions at all.

'I've arranged cover at work for seven days and business class helps.'

Mia nodded. 'I'll bet.'

'John said his housekeeper, Gladys someone...'

'Henderson,' Mia supplied. The spritely sixty-year-old cleaned their apartment too.

'Yes, that's her. She's going to keep an eye on the apartment for me.'

'Okay.' Mia waited for him to say more. Or to pick up his bags and leave. He didn't. She frowned. 'Why are you here, Luca?' she asked wearily.

Luca put his hand in his pocket. 'To thank you.' He looked at her intently, her fluffy pink dressing gown somehow just as sexy as the winter coat from last night. 'You were right. I needed to do this.'

Mia shrugged. 'No worries.'

He chose his next words carefully. Normally he didn't have to give 'the speech' but Mia was different. Somehow she'd got past the barriers that he'd erected since Marissa and she deserved him to be straight with her.

He wanted her to know that it wasn't her—it was him.

He just didn't do emotional connections and he especially didn't need that baggage now, heading off to face some pretty big demons.

He was surprised, though, at how hard the words were to say. At his reticence.

'I know I wasn't good company this morning and—'

'It's okay, Luca,' Mia interrupted, knowing from his eyes what he was going to say and suddenly not wanting to hear the words come from his mouth. 'I get it. You and I were always just a one-time thing that went on for longer than it should have. Neither of us do this sort of thing. I think we can just walk away and chalk it up to experience.'

Luca pursed his lips. It was an easy out for him but, still, her even easier acceptance rankled. It shouldn't have. It should have been a relief.

But it wasn't.

'I think it's best,' he murmured.

It was. It had to be.

'Of course,' she assured him. So why didn't it feel like it? Why did she feel worse than she had all day?

They stood in the doorway, looking at each other for a moment, not speaking. *It was for the best. It was.*

'I'm sorry.' Luca grimaced, checking his watch. 'I have to go, I have a taxi waiting.'

Mia nodded, her heart hammering in her chest. 'Sure. I'll see you when you get back,' she said. 'At work.'

'Yes,' he agreed, fighting the urge to seize her in his arms and kiss her and the even more bizarre urge to ask her to go with him.

To complicate it much more than it already was.

'At work,' he repeated. Then he turned away, picked up his bag and strode down the corridor to the lift, not daring to look back.

Mia stared after him, watching until he disappeared.

It—whatever *it* was—was over. She should be over the moon.

She wasn't.

'That seemed pretty intense. What was it about?' Evie asked.

Mia swivelled her head to find her friend walking towards her. At least she finally looked interested in something else other than overdosing on salt and vinegar chips and Boston pub life.

'Nothing,' Mia said, recovering sufficiently to withdraw into the warm apartment and shut the door.

'Didn't look like nothing to me,' Evie mused.

'It is now,' Mia assured her.

For five days and nights, despite her every effort not to, Mia thought of Luca constantly. Her feelings fluctuated wildly from complete understanding and agreement with their decision to walk away from each other, to worry about how it was all panning out in Marsala, to an uncharacteristic yearning for something she couldn't even put her finger on.

Add to that a healthy dose of sexual frustration from vivid dreams and Mia was a wreck.

The dreams were the worst.

Happily-ever-after fantasies—erotic one moment, white-wedding poignant the next. They woke her often, rendering her perpetually tired. And cranky. The staff avoided her. Her patients asked the nurses their questions. Even Evie stayed out of her way.

In fact, by day five her best friend was suggesting she burn off some of the bitch with a good old-fashioned bar pick-up somewhere.

Then, on the sixth night, Luca came striding into the

department at almost midnight. His luscious wavy hair, speckled with raindrops from the stormy weather outside, looked like it had hadn't seen a comb in a while and it was the first time she'd seen him unshaven.

He looked like hell.

And her body responded with a primal lurch.

If anything, with the heavy growth of blue-black stubble and the wicked way he filled out a pair of jeans, he looked more like the devil she'd first pegged him as than ever before.

But she knew him much better now.

Well…better than she had, anyway.

'Luca?' Her heart pounded in her chest. Damn it, this wasn't how she'd planned on greeting him on his return. Where was her polite smile and cool nod? 'You're not due back until tomorrow!'

Luca ran a hand through his already unruly hair. She was a sight for sore eyes. It had been a harrowing time in Sicily and even though they weren't together—had never really been together—he wanted to drag her to the on-call room and get lost in her for a little while.

Just one more time.

'I couldn't sleep and I heard the ambulances.' He shrugged. 'Thought I'd drop by and see if you guys needed a hand.'

Mia saw the flash of desire in his deep dark eyes, like a candle in a well, and felt it slug her right in the belly. She was grateful for the bustle of the department around them. If he'd come to her door, she'd have been lost in a look like that. Their parting conversation from six days ago smothered by a fierce surge of lust and a strong urge for privacy.

She blinked, taking a mental step backwards. 'You look tired. Are you up to it?'

'I'm fine.'

Mia raised an eyebrow. 'You don't look it.'

Luca waved a dismissive hand. 'I'm exhausted and my body clock's screwed up but I'm not sleepy. In fact, I'm buzzing. I'm good to work.'

Mia scrutinised him for a moment but that was just plain dangerous. Besides, she understood how jet-lag could mess with your body but have the opposite effect on your brain. And they were pretty slammed at the moment.

'Okay, sure. There was an industrial fire with several burn victims, we're down a couple of nurses and Evie's attending an arrest on one of the wards. It's bedlam.'

He nodded. 'Okay.'

She waited for him to move on, brush past her, leap into action, but he didn't. He just stood looking at her, weary and subdued. 'How…how was it?'

Not that she cared. Not that she wanted to know.

Luca rubbed at his stubble. 'Bad.' A nurse bustled past them.

Mia heard the low accented rumble right down to her toes. 'Do you want to talk about it?'

What the hell?

She didn't want him to talk about it. She didn't want to listen. She didn't want to know. The only thing she was interested in was the magic he could wreak on her body.

And even that was now off limits.

His life was none of her damn business and she liked it that way!

Luca shook his head. He didn't. He really, really

didn't. Three days of dealing with family history had been enough to bear, without rehashing it. What he wanted was to forget it. Lay her down and let their magic take him somewhere else.

A place where he wasn't a hormone-driven, starry-eyed sixteen-year-old. Where he hadn't got his brother's girlfriend—now wife—pregnant. A place where there were no toxic family relationships, where he hadn't let anyone down, where no one disapproved.

And Mia was the perfect woman for that. Gorgeous, sexually uninhibited and emotionally unavailable.

That's what he needed. Talking—not so much.

'I just need to work.'

Mia nodded. 'Cubicle two.' And held her breath as Luca brushed past her.

Two hours later the department had quietened down. The minor burn victims had been triaged, assessed and transferred to the burns unit. Of the two more serious burns, one had gone to Theatre, the other to ICU.

Mia was able to breathe again. To think of something other than ABCs and burns percentages and fluid requirements. She glanced at Luca, who was writing in a chart. He glanced up at the same time and the heat flaring between them could have lit the Sydney Harbour Bridge for all eternity.

Okay. *Enough.* They'd been lovers—briefly. That was all and now it was over. They'd agreed. This… sexual ESP stuff couldn't go on.

It just couldn't.

She stood. 'Can I speak with you please, Dr di Angelo?' she asked quietly, looking around her at the completely disinterested staff going about their own business.

Luca looked up at her, the quiet steel in her voice at odds with the heat in her eyes. 'On-call room?'

Mia felt the kick in her pulse. *The things they'd done in that on-call room...* But the fact was that their privacy was absolute there—the perfect place to tell him this couldn't go on.

'Sure.'

Mia turned and led the way on very shaky legs, hyper-aware of his gaze glued to her back. When she finally reached her destination she headed straight for the kitchenette and grabbed two mugs, absently going about the business of fixing them coffee. She heard the door shut behind her. Then lock. She was conscious of Luca leaning against it, watching her.

Mia turned to face him, her butt resting against the sink. He looked dark and wild and every fibre of her being wanted to melt into his arms. 'We agreed not to do this any more.'

Luca hung onto the doorknob. She was right. They had. But he'd thought of nothing else for the last few hours. Since returning home. Hell, since leaving. And he'd happily walk away. But he needed tonight.

He didn't know why. He just knew he did.

'I know.'

Mia shook her head emphatically. 'I don't do this, Luca. We,' she wagged her finger back and forth between the two of them. 'We don't do this.'

Luca pushed away from the door and prowled over, halting in front of her. Close enough to see the frantic flicker of the pulse at the base of her throat, the flare of her nostrils, the dilation of her pupils.

'I know.'

Mia felt the rumble of his voice curl her toes. Lust, full and throaty and undisguised, thickened his accent. He crowded her against the sink and her fingers automatically curled into the sleeves of his shirt. Their bodies touched from hip to shoulder and it felt so good she almost whimpered.

Mia swallowed and clawed desperately for some self-control. 'We're alike, you and I, Luca. We have scars… trust issues. We guard our hearts. We don't get involved. It's why we're emergency doctors—patch 'em up and ship 'em out, right? No time to get involved. It's who we are.'

Luca looked deep into her eyes. 'Who are you trying to convince Mia—me or yourself?'

Mia glared at him. Damn it, she was trying to walk this thing back. *Why wasn't he meeting her halfway?* Why was he trying to change the boundaries he'd set before he'd left? Damn it all, the boundaries he lived by.

They both lived by.

'Am I wrong?' she challenged.

Luca shook his head. 'No.' In fact, she was one hundred per cent accurate. But that didn't stop the primal beat of a jungle drum thrumming through his blood. His gaze brushed her mouth. 'But I need this. I wish I didn't. But I do.'

He placed a hand on the cold stainless-steel of the sink either side of her and dropped his head, claiming her mouth on a muffled groan. She opened for him instantly, her tongue seeking his, and his barely leashed desire blazed to life with all the heat and intensity of a solar flare.

His hands skimmed up her body and buried themselves in her hair, pulling at the band tying it back, releasing it in a tumble of blonde, his fingers seeking the spot where nape met scalp. Her corresponding moan went straight to his groin.

Yes, yes, yes. This was what he needed. A place to feel good, to feel like a successful, virile man again instead of a home-wrecking boy. A place to forget.

He pulled away from the softness of her mouth to explore the delights of her neck. 'I missed you,' he murmured against the pulse fluttering in her throat.

Because he had. Thoughts of her had been his constant companion while he'd been away. Had often been his only relief from what had been a tense and stilted time.

His hands left her hair, travelled to her hips, gripping them hard as he lifted her onto the narrow edge of the sink, stepped between her legs, forcing them apart, grinding his monster erection against the place where he knew it fitted perfectly.

Mia gasped as her hips responded to the blatant invitation. She wanted him inside her so badly she could practically feel his hardness stretching her.

Here on the sink. In the on-call room. With the bustle of an entire emergency department just outside the door.

This was madness!

'Luca, stop, no, please, stop.'

She pushed at his shoulders as his tongue laved a wet track from her ear to her collarbone. Her heart pounded in her ears and for an insane moment she thought it was someone pounding against the door. 'We really need to stop this.'

Luca pulled away, his chest heaving. 'If you want me to stop, I'll stop.' His breath sawed in and out of his chest as he stared into blue eyes that were hazy with lust. He pulled her in tight to his hips. 'But I don't think you really want me to.'

Mia's head was spinning, her chest was bursting, her belly was clenched in a tight knot. Common sense warred with primal craving. He rotated his hips against hers and she bit down a moan.

To hell with it. She wanted it, needed it—needed him—too much to deny it.

'This is it, Luca. After this, there is no more.'

The words were barely out before Luca was whispering, 'Done,' and reclaiming her mouth.

Mia welcomed the sweep of his tongue and the triumphant noise at the back of his throat when she opened to his long, deep, hot kiss. She especially welcomed his harsh intake of breath as her hands found his zipper and tugged it down.

'Wrap your legs around me,' he murmured, scooping her hips off the edge and grasping her buttocks firmly in his hands as he hauled her off the sink and headed for one of the rooms. Her ankles locked around his waist and he almost stumbled as her hands continued their quest to get behind his zip while her tongue flicked at the pulse thudding at the base of his throat.

He kicked the door shut behind them and tumbled them onto the couch her legs wide, her knees bent, his hips perfectly aligned with hers. His shirt was off in five seconds. Hers followed closely after.

And then a pager beeped.

Mia froze. Luca cursed in his mother tongue.

They both lay there for a few seconds, not moving,

their frantic breath and the trilling of a pager the only sound in the room.

Mia pushed against Luca's shoulders. 'Let me up,' she requested, hating how husky her voice sounded.

Luca pushed off her, sitting back on the couch, his chest naked, his fly gaping open. He raked a hand through his hair while Mia ripped the pager off her waistband and read the liquid crystal display. 'Chopper retrieval,' she relayed. 'MVA near the Blue Mountains.'

She swung herself into a sitting position, her scrambled thoughts sluggish as she tried to switch into medical mode. Luca handed over her shirt and she looked at it absently for a moment before realising she was sitting there in her bra and a pair of jeans.

Too close to Luca for comfort, she stood and fixed her clothing. She straightened her shoulders, pulled her hair back, cleared her throat. She headed for the door and paused with her hand on the knob. 'I'd better go.'

Luca watched her from the sofa. 'This isn't over, Mia.'

Mia knew they couldn't keep doing this. Whatever the two of them were doing had overstepped both their boundaries and all this sexual gratification was doing was prolonging the inevitable. If they'd been meant to be together one last time, they wouldn't have been interrupted.

The pager was a sign from the universe.

'Yes, it is,' she said without looking back, and then swept from the room.

Luca watched her disappear and knew in his bones that there would be no changing her mind. It shouldn't have mattered. He'd done this dozens of times with dozens of women. Had had a good time for a while then walked away without looking back.

No harm, no foul.

Except it did matter. Somehow these past weeks with Mia had come to mean more than a sexual pressure valve.

Mia mattered.

CHAPTER NINE

TWENTY minutes later Mia and Luca were sitting opposite each other strapped into the rescue helicopter, watching the rooftop helipad lights bend and twist as they refracted through the raindrops clinging to the chopper's windows. Luca had volunteered to go with her due to the shortage of nurses in the department and the ICU retrieval team also being out on a call.

'Okay, folks, welcome to Brian Air. Please ensure your tray tables are in an upright position and your seat belts are fastened low and tight. It's going to be an interesting ride.'

Mia grinned at the amplified patter in her earphones despite the tension she felt at sitting opposite a man she'd been mere minutes away from feeling deep inside her. Brian was one of the pilots who had been flying rescue choppers for ever and his skill and experience were much appreciated on a stormy night.

Even his sense of humour.

'Please don't tell me we're heading into a storm, Brian.'

'Would I do that to you, Mia, my lovely?'

Luca gritted his teeth at the easy banter. He had a sudden urge to break something of Brian's. Something non-essential, of course. He still had to be able to fly the damn chopper.

'There is some storm activity but I'll be skirting around it. Safe as houses. Cross my heart. Would I lie to you?'

Mia laughed. 'You? Never.'

Brian laughed back. 'Got yourself a man yet?'

Mia's smile died, her gaze locking with Luca's. 'I'm too busy for a man.'

Brian tsked into his headset. 'Now, if only I was twenty years younger. What's wrong with men these days, Luca? Are they blind?'

Mia tried to look away from him but Luca's brooding gaze held her captive.

'Not all of us,' Luca murmured.

Mia pursed her lips. 'You know me, Brian—don't like to be tied down.'

Luca had no doubt the words were for his benefit and he switched off to the patter as he shifted his gaze from Mia to the now far-away lights of Sydney. The steady beat of the rotors above him echoed the thud of his heart beat as he tried to catalogue the swirl of alien feelings churning in his gut.

In less than two months Dr Mia McKenzie had taken over his life. And he wasn't sure exactly when it had happened. All he knew *for sure* was that the thought of never being with her again was not one he relished.

She'd been the one he'd thought of while he'd been away. Not the air hostess in business class who'd slipped him her card. Not the many beautiful Sicilian women who had smiled at him with frank interest on the streets of Marsala. Not even Marissa, his brother's wife, the woman he'd foolishly thought himself in love with all those years ago.

Mia. It had been Mia who he'd thought of. Mia he'd picked up the phone to ring after his brother had paid him a visit at his hotel and told him to go home. *And then put down again.* Mia who he'd credited as he'd talked to his grandmother standing by her fresh grave after the other mourners had left. Mia who had got him through a killer flight as he'd fantasised about their reunion.

He stole a glance at her as she flicked through the retrieval paperwork balanced on a clipboard on her lap. She was gorgeous even in a big yellow helmet that made her look as if she was trapped inside a giant insect eye and flight overalls that seemed two sizes too big for her.

He looked away again as the insanity of it all hit him. He'd always been able to walk away. Always. None of this made sense.

And none of it made him happy.

It was official—he was having a truly hellish week.

'So the ambulance crew on scene have the patient stabilised and ready for transport,' Mia said, conscious of his eyes on her and desperate to get back to a professional footing after their *coitus interruptus.*

Their patient had suspected spinal injuries requiring rapid air evacuation for maximum treatment success and that's what she needed to focus on.

Luca nodded. 'Should just be able to scoop and run.'

Mia hoped so. The rain had picked up and the chopper seemed to be being buffeted by some decent wind. She could see lightning in the distance and guessed that was the storm they were skirting around. At the best of times Mia wasn't the greatest flyer in the world and she knew that Brian wouldn't be flying if he didn't think it was safe but the sooner they were back at The Harbour in one piece, the better. And then there was Luca, sitting opposite her, watching her with brooding eyes and causing another kind of storm. Inside her. She'd never met a man she couldn't handle and she hated it that she couldn't shake him. From her thoughts. Her dreams.

Her daydreams!

'Think I might get a bit of shut-eye,' she said into her mike. It was, after all, nearly three in the morning and she'd long ago learned the value of power-napping.

She didn't wait for anyone's permission, just closed her eyes. And dreamed of Luca.

A loud bang woke her with a start fifteen minutes later. The chopper spun wildly and her head was filled with Brian swearing and putting out a mayday call. Her eyes flew to the man opposite her. 'Luca?'

Luca saw alarm and fear in her eyes and felt his own pulse leap as the helicopter seemed to be losing altitude as it spun. 'Brian?' He spoke into his headphones. 'What's happening?'

'Lightning took out the tail rotor,' Brian said calmly, while desperately trying to regain control of the spiralling chopper.

'I thought you said you were skirting around the storm?' Mia said above the noise of her pistoning heart and the whine of the labouring engine. She braced one hand against the stretcher beside her and the other against the aircraft shell to steady herself in the midst of the crazy spinning.

'I am. Mother nature can be a bitch like that sometimes.'

How was it possible that Brian could even sound upbeat during a mid-air emergency?

'Are we going to crash?' she asked.

'Hell, yeah,' Brian said matter-of-factly. 'Brace yourselves, guys, we're over national park and there're a lot of trees down there.'

Mia tamped down on the rather alien urge to become hysterical. It wasn't what she usually did in a crisis but, hell, they were going to crash. She was twenty-nine and she was going to die. She hadn't witnessed the northern lights. She hadn't bought herself that cute little retro convertible. She hadn't been to the ballet.

She hadn't been in love.

Except she had, of course.

And the man she loved was going to die with her.

Her gaze locked with Luca's. What a really, really horrible time for such a profound revelation. No time to hug it to herself like a delicious little secret.

'Oh, God,' Mia whispered, her throat suddenly as dry as ash, her eyes trying to take in every detail of Luca's face.

'It's going to be okay, Mia,' Luca said.

He reached out his hand, hoping his grandmother was out there somewhere watching over them. He was damned if he was going to die before telling Mia how he felt about her.

Whatever the hell that was.

If he'd learned anything this past week it was that life was short and you couldn't live in the past.

Mia slipped her hand into his and gripped tight. It was cold and she was trembling and he'd have given anything to erase the glimpse of mortality he could see in her eyes.

'Just because we crash it doesn't mean we're going to die. Does it, Brian?' Luca queried.

He was calm, so bloody calm. How could Luca be this calm as the helicopter spiralled out of control in a death plunge? Her brain was spinning just as wildly. Desperately trying to remember helicopter crash statistics while grappling with regret that she wasn't closer to her parents and sorrow that her fledgling love for Luca was going to be snuffed out before she'd even had the chance to explore it.

'Not on my watch,' Brian chirped. 'Okay, guys, hold tight. Prepare for impact.'

Mia squeezed Luca's hand hard. 'I've never seen *Swan Lake*.'

Luca smiled at her. 'When this is over, we'll go and see it together.'

There was no time for her to smile back. The crippled chopper hit trees with a violent jolt, halting the rapid downward spiral most effectively. Mia squeezed her eyes shut as the impact raced through her body like a giant shock wave. She vaguely heard cracking glass, a loud expletive followed by a guttural cry from Brian and then nothing other than the screech and grind of the rotors could be heard as they sliced through the canopy. Mia, eyes still shut, hit her head several times against the shell of the cabin and she was grateful for her helmet as the chopper lurched and listed, dropping a little then stopping then dropping again as the branches beneath buckled beneath its weight before it finally came to a shuddering halt.

After a good twenty seconds of no movement, Mia cracked open an eye. She could hear Brian talking to Air Control, she could smell rain and fuel and eucalyptus, she could feel the wind buffeting the chopper and hear it whistling inside the cabin. Her eyes adjusted to the sudden darkness and she could see Luca sitting opposite, wonderfully intact.

She was alive. *They were all alive!*

'You okay?' Luca asked.

Mia thought about it for a moment. Everything felt fine. She nodded. 'Yes…I think. You?'

Luca nodded back. 'Yes.' And then he grinned. '*Swan Lake,* here we come.'

Mia grinned back. Her first instinct, to throw herself at him, was pulled up short by a moan coming from the front.

'Brian? Are you okay?' Luca asked.

'Leg's busted,' the pilot panted as he killed the engine.

Luca glanced at Mia. The pain in Brian's voice was obvious. 'Is that a guess or can you see it?'

Brian swore again. 'Tree branch breached the cab, drove into my leg. I can see the bones.'

They exchanged glances again. Luca felt a moment of guilt at his earlier wish that Brian would break something. 'Any other injuries?'

'Nope. Don't think so.'

Luca wasn't totally reassured. Often people could have wounds they weren't even aware of if there was one overriding painful injury.

'Okay, so we need to get you out of there onto the stretcher so we can splint your leg and give you something for the pain. Lucky for you, you crashlanded a mini emergency ward, they have all the best drugs.'

Brian gave a half laugh, half snort at Luca's attempt

to keep things light. 'Ah. You cottoned onto my das-tardly plan.'

Luca unbuckled. Mia followed.

'Wait,' Brian called out. 'We need to assess how this bird's being supported. I don't know how precarious it is and moving around could dislodge it. I'd hate to survive the first crash only to be killed on impact with the ground.'

Luca paused. He could tell that Brian was trying to make light of the situation but he also knew that Brian was still thinking like a pilot. Which, given his horrific injury, was amazing.

'Okay,' Luca said. 'How do we do that?'

'If you can open your door safely, grab the torch and have a look out, see if you can see what's support-ing us. But move carefully until we know. The crash would have activated our emergency locator transmit-ter so Air Control will know where we are but they'll want a sit rep—once we know what we're up against, I'll let them know.'

Luca glanced at Mia. The chopper had come to a stop in a reasonably level position with a slight tilt to the left so he was pretty certain that movement wouldn't be an issue but that all depended on what was beneath them.

'Buckle up,' he said as he reached for the torch strapped to the cabin above his head and gently re-moved it.

Mia felt a trickle of dread drip down her spine. 'Be careful.'

Luca nodded, aware that they might well be precari-ously balanced and not keen to be the one that upset the apple cart. It was good to know that their ELT had been activated and that help would no doubt soon be on its way. But Brian, while he was being very stoic, needed urgent medical attention, so they couldn't just sit around and wait.

He swivelled in his seat and shone the torch out the window. Through the now driving rain he could see that the door appeared to be free of any vegetation so he gingerly reached for the handle and gently eased it open. The freezing rain assaulted him almost immediately as he carefully lowered himself to the floor of the cabin, hung his head out and shone the torch under the chopper.

They appeared to be wedged between three massive looking tree trunks huddled together. The bottom of the cabin was supported by sturdy interwoven branches which appeared knotted. The tail also seemed wedged between two trunks further back.

Luca shone the torch down towards the forest floor. Whether it was the rain or the dark or the sheer distance, he couldn't make it out. It was nothing but a swirling abyss of cloud and night.

He crawled back in and gently shut the door. His overalls were soaked around the shoulders and the part of his face not protected by the helmet was as wet as if he'd just stepped out of the shower.

He scrambled to his feet and gave a very slight experimental bounce. When the chopper stayed firm he gave another bigger one. 'I think it's fine.'

He relayed the info to Brian who spoke with Air Control. Luca experimented some more, shifting slowly and carefully around the cramped confines of the chopper, which was hardly made for ease of movement anyway.

It seemed stable and he let out a little sigh of relief.

'Bad news.' Brian's voice interrupted Luca. 'The weather has worsened. High winds and driving rain are going to make rescue impossible for a while. It's too dangerous to send another chopper and a winch crew. Meteorology think the system's going to hang around for quite a few more hours so we're stuck up this tree until daylight. Like the bloody Swiss Family Robinson.'

Mia heard Brian laugh at his own joke then suck in a breath on a deep guttural groan.

'We've got to see to him,' she said.

Luca nodded. 'I think the chopper's stable enough to drag him out of his seat and onto the stretcher. It's going to hurt, though.'

Mia nodded grimly. Hell, yeah. 'We could get him to splint his leg first—we carry vacuum splints—it might help a bit.'

Luca nodded. 'Okay. Let's do it. Unbuckle, but slowly. And leave your helmet on. Let's make sure this bird can take both of us moving around before we get too carried away.'

Mia unbuckled and stood slowly. Luca held out his hand and she glanced at him as she took it.

'You're freezing,' he murmured, enclosing her hand within his.

Mia was surprised to realise she was—she'd been in survival mode and hadn't realised it. 'The wind's getting in somewhere,' she said absently, caught up in the warmth of his hand.

Despite how soaked his shoulders and arms were, his hands were like a toasty pair of gloves. In fact, his mere presence was like a beacon of light in this cold, dark, scary scenario they'd landed in.

Luca was here and he was warm and solid and one hundred per cent in control.

'Near Brian, I think,' Luca murmured, steadying her. 'Grab the splint,' he said. 'Slow and easy. I don't know how much weight distribution is aiding stability.'

Mia nodded and reluctantly let go of Luca's hand. She'd felt safe under the influence of his touch. Which made no sense. They were still stuck up a tree. In a helicopter. In the middle of a storm.

Which just went to prove what she'd always thought— love was crazy!

She took a tentative step and then another towards the storage cupboard. Like boats, helicopters made excellent use of space and Mia knew what was in every nook and cranny. The floor felt solid beneath her as she inched her way closer.

She grabbed the splint and the pump and turned to face Luca. 'What now?'

He held out his hand and she passed him the gear. He gestured her close. 'I'm going to drag him out from behind. You stand by at the stretcher for when he's out. Let's get an IV going and give him some morph.'

Mia looked at the cramped confines of the single pilot's seat. The end of the stretcher protruded into the front cab area where in most commercial choppers there would have been a second seat.

'Are you going to be able to manoeuvre him out from behind?'

Luca grimaced. 'I hope so. I'm not sure how stable the chopper will be if I have to climb up onto the stretcher and pull him from there. The tail's wedged fairly solidly so I doubt it'll tip backwards. I'm not so sure it won't tip forward.'

Mia swallowed. So this was the meaning of being stuck between a rock and a hard place. But Luca seemed so confident—like GI Joe, Action Man and Inspector Gadget all rolled into one.

'It's going to be fine, Mia.' He smiled. She returned his smile with one that was suddenly wobbly and thanked any and all deities out there that if she'd had to be in a helicopter crash, at least Luca had been with her.

'Okay. Let's do it.'

Twenty minutes later, after a lot of effort and pain, Brian was on the stretcher, an IV had been inserted, fluids were running, nasal prongs with a trickle of oxygen had been applied and, because they could, he was being monitored. His badly fractured leg had been left in the splint and he'd drifted off to sleep on a morphine cloud.

Finally they both settled back into their seats. The wind howled around the chopper and whistled through the shattered glass at the front. She could feel the slight shuddering of the aircraft as the wind buffeted it from what seemed like all directions. The steady beep, beep, beep of the monitor seemed alien amidst the wild brutality of Mother Nature.

'How long do you think the oxygen will last?' Mia asked into the growing silence.

She knew that Brian didn't really need it but she was aware it was a finite commodity and that they had no idea how long they'd be there. They'd completed a thorough primary and secondary survey of Brian's injuries but what if they'd missed something? What if his condition worsened?

'Quite a few hours, I expect. It's only running at one litre.'

Mia nodded. Would that be enough? How long would it be before they were rescued? The way the wind howled and the rain beat incessantly against the window, it didn't look like any time soon.

She tried really hard not to think about the precariousness of the situation. Their position might feel stable enough but that didn't alter the fact that they were still in a great deal of danger.

'So, now what?' Mia asked.

'We should get some sleep too,' Luca said into the silence.

Mia shook her head, reaching across to feel once again for the pulses in Brian's foot. They were there but feeble and Mia guessed the injury was compromising the blood flow lower. 'I'm worried about the circulation,' Mia murmured. 'It'd be awful to survive a crash like this then go on to lose your leg.'

Luca, who was worried too, gave her a reassuring smile. 'Hopefully we'll be out of here before it comes to that.'

Mia nodded. Suddenly aware she was still wearing her helmet, she pulled it off.

Luca placed a stilling hand on her forearm. 'You should leave it on,' he said.

Mia shook her hair free and finger-combed it. 'I'll feel ridiculous sitting here for the next who knows how long in this stupid helmet.'

Luca sought her gaze. 'If whatever's supporting us gives way, that helmet could be your lifeline.'

Mia glanced away from the stark reality she saw in his deep, dark eyes. 'Well, I doubt very much it'll prevent my neck from being broken, which is the most likely outcome if this thing plummets to the ground.'

Luca knew she was right. Spinal compression injury would be the true killer. That and the many other possibilities in between flitted through his mind as he watched Mia with a growing sense of helplessness.

He hated being powerless to affect change in this situation. That all three of them were dependent on things outside his control—the weather, branch structure, the expertise of others.

He'd been taking care of himself for a long time now. So, he suspected, had she. This kind of impotence was reminiscent of his past. And he'd had a little too much of that already this last week.

He took off his own helmet and ruffled his hair.

'We're going to be fine,' he murmured. If he had to hold this helicopter in place through sheer force of will, he would. *He wouldn't let Mia down.* He tapped the top of her helmet. 'Keep it close.'

Mia nodded. 'I don't suppose Air Control said what was happening with the patient we're supposed to be evac'ing?' Luca had talked with Air Control while she'd been inserting the IV.

'They're coming in by road. No choice now.'

Mia knew that would be an hour or so's drive in these treacherous weather conditions, even with lights and sirens. The mountain roads were dangerous when wet and low cloud would further inhibit speed.

'Hopefully the patient's spinal condition is minor,' Mia commented, rubbing absently at her arms. Although she doubted very much they would have been sent out on such a night for a chipped vertebra.

'You cold?' Luca asked.

'A little,' she admitted. The breached cabin was a perfect conduit for the freezing wind and the temperature inside the crippled aircraft had dropped considerably.

They'd covered Brian in a space blanket but now her adrenaline had settled and their activity had ceased she was starting to feel cold gnawing at her arms. 'You must be too,' Mia said. 'Your overalls are wet around your shoulders and chest.'

Luca wasn't really. His body was still on high alert, his metabolic rate steaming along like a whistling kettle. But they were probably going to be there for a while...

He leaned across and dragged a pack out from under the stretcher, locating the stash of space blankets folded neatly into playing-card-sized packaging.

'Here,' he said, passing her one. Then he opened another and unfolded it. The thin, metallic, foil material crinkled noisily, like a chocolate wrapper, as he proceeded to scrunch it up.

'What are you doing?' Mia asked as she unfolded hers and stood so she could wrap it around her entire body.

'I'm going to plug the hole with it,' Luca murmured.

'Ah...good thinking,' she said as she moved aside to give him more room to manoeuvre.

Luca carefully leaned over Brian's seat and gingerly stuffed the whistling hole with the scrunched-up foil blanket. 'That should do it,' he said, standing back to admire his handiwork.

'Sounds like it,' Mia agreed as the whistling magically stopped.

He smiled down at her and in the confines of the helicopter a hunched Luca seemed to take up all the space.

She hadn't had time to think about her startling revelation from earlier, but now it was all she could think about.

She was in love with Luca di Angelo.

For better or worse. And surely this *had* to be the worst?

'It's going to be okay,' Luca murmured, lifting his hand to cup her cheek. 'You're going to be okay.'

Mia wasn't sure if she'd ever be okay again. She'd gone and done something she'd sworn she never would—fallen in love. How could life ever be okay? How could it ever be the same?

The air seemed to thicken as they stood hunched over in the middle of the helicopter, staring at each other. The howl of the wind and the steady beeping of the heart-rate monitor twirled around them like a symphony.

Brian chose that moment to stir, crinkling the space blanket and setting off the monitor alarm. Luca's hand dropped as he started guiltily and immediately switched his attention to the stretcher.

Luca placed his hand on the pilot's shoulder. 'Hurting, Brian?'

Brian's eyes drifted open and he gave them a goofy smile. 'Nope. Everything ish wonderfullll,' he slurred. 'That morphine is gooood stuff.' And his eyes drifted shut again.

Mia, who was once again checking Brian's foot pulses, smiled. Obviously the pain relief was working.

'How are they?' Luca asked.

'The same, I think. The foot seems a little cooler, though.'

They resumed their seats, Luca wrapping himself in a space blanket as well. He checked his watch. 'Nearly four-thirty,' he said as he peered out the rain-spattered window.

They sat in silence for some minutes, both looking out at the watery blackness. 'This wasn't quite how I imagined my first visit to the Blue Mountains would pan out,' Luca murmured.

Mia's gaze slid from the window to his profile. 'I recommend driving next time.'

There was a pause as their eyes met and then they both laughed. Mia's stomach rumbled. 'Are you hungry?' She grabbed her backpack from its hidey-hole. The foil of the space blanket crinkled with her every movement. 'There's usually some exceedingly fattening, sugar-loaded snacks in here.'

She gave a triumphant whoop when she located two chocolate bars and handed him one. She tore off her wrapper and sighed as she savoured that first sinful bite. 'To think, this could be the last chocolate I ever eat.'

Luca glanced at her sharply. 'Don't talk like that.'

Mia shrugged as the other lasts competed for equal placing. Last time smelling eucalyptus. Last time seeing rain.

Last time being with Luca.

She wondered if she confessed to these crazy new feelings whether Luca would pretend that he reciprocated. He could renege when they were safely back in Sydney, she wouldn't hold him to it, but if she was about to meet her fate then…why not utter the words?

Because she didn't want her last moments filled with an awkward silence and an even more awkward Luca trying to figure out how to let her down gently before they crashed to a fiery death.

Or worse—watch him lie to her.

Yes, he wanted her. But that was different from love. And, faced with her own mortality, nothing less would do.

She sighed again. 'Just being realistic.'

Luca shook his head. 'We're in a stable position. Air Control has our ELT signal. We just need to wait out the weather and then they'll get us out of here as soon as they can.'

Mia nodded. Listening to the sure, steady note in his voice, she believed him. 'I know.'

They finished their chocolate serenaded by the moaning wind and the rhythmic beeping of the monitor. Luca shut his eyes briefly and let his head flop back against the headrest. The fine crinkle of the space blanket sounded like crickets chirping as he shifted to get comfortable, stretching his long legs out into the confined space.

His legs brushed hers and he lifted his head. 'Sorry.' He grimaced as he shifted them slightly to one side.

'It's fine,' she murmured.

Their gazes locked and for the longest moment they just sat and watched each other. Luca was the first to break the connection.

'So…you've never seen *Swan Lake*?'

Mia didn't say anything for a minute. Then she just shook her head. 'Have you?'

He nodded. 'My grandmother adored things like that. Opera was her first love but she enjoyed ballet too. And she insisted we all be well versed.' He smiled at the memory. 'She took me and my sisters to Rome when I was twelve because it was playing at the Teatro dell'Opera.'

Mia remembered he'd mentioned having sisters before. She heard the affection in his voice and felt a corresponding ache of longing deep inside. Her life had been far from family outings to the opera and ballet.

'You have three sisters, right?'

'Yes.' He toyed with leaving it at that but was surprised by the urge to confess all. 'And a brother.'

His accent thickened and Mia heard the regret in every syllable. He'd mentioned he'd been ostracised and she could hear the pain in every husky nuance. How terrible to have lost an entire extended family. Two people had been hard enough.

'What happened, Luca?'

She'd told him she hadn't wanted to know. And she hadn't. But that was before feeling the power of a love so deep that, even now, despite its newness, it was nestling in to her bones, bedding in for the long haul.

Now she wanted to know everything about him.

She wanted to know it all.

Luca hesitated at her soft enquiry, knowing the answer involved a trip down memory lane. And he'd just flown halfway round the world to come back from there. But somehow, with his recent trip back to the scene of the crime and the potentially dire situation they were in, it didn't seem so confronting.

In fact, it seemed kind of cathartic.

And in this strange metal cocoon, perched in the treetops of an ancient forest, it seemed as if they were the only two people in the entire world. Despite the beeping of Brian's monitor, the occasional staccato chatter from the radio and the ever-present potential for disaster, the atmosphere was intimate.

Maybe it was the rain—the whole dark, stormy night

thing—but somehow the mood was conducive to confidences and deep dark secrets.

And it was Mia. The one woman he instinctively knew would understand. But where did he start?

CHAPTER TEN

M<small>IA</small> watched and waited. She could see Luca was grappling with some demons and she held her breath, hoping like crazy he'd open up to her.

'I fell in love for the first time…' Luca paused. 'The only time…when I was sixteen.'

Mia steeled herself against the jab to her chest. He seemed so definite. So absolute.

He snorted. 'At least, I thought I had. I think lust or infatuation is probably more appropriate when I think about it now.'

Mia tried to ignore how the spike of jealousy hurt. *It was an ancient love affair, for crying out loud!*

'She must have been a hell of a girl,' she said, forcing lightness to her tone, and turned to look out the window because she couldn't bear to see what love looked like in his eyes. Not when it was for another woman.

He nodded. 'Oh, yes. Her family was an old, important family in Sicily and our two families had had a deep and abiding friendship for generations. She was promised to my brother.'

Mia's gaze snapped back to his. 'Promised? Like an arranged marriage?'

Luca smiled at her shock. 'Yes, Mia. An arranged marriage. This is Sicily where the old ways still rule.'

Mia blinked at the strange concept. 'But…you fell in love with her instead?'

Luca shook his head. 'As well.'

Oh. Mia felt goose-bumps on her arms as if the wind had found its way in again and blown right up beneath the blanket. There was nothing as heart-wrenching as brother against brother. She hunched into the space blanket a little more with a corresponding ruffle. 'Ah.'

Luca gave a grim nod. 'Yes. Ah.'

She quirked an eyebrow. 'Were there pistols at dawn?' she joked.

Luca gave a half-smile. 'No. That might have been quicker.'

Mia sobered. 'It was bad.' She wasn't sure if it was a question or a statement.

Luca nodded. 'Marissa and Carlos had a tempestuous relationship. He was twenty-three and she was eighteen when the engagement became official. He worked in Rome and was away frequently so Marissa and I hung out a lot. And when they were together they argued frequently then made up again. I think they both loved the drama of it all. And I…'

Luca paused as he remembered how love-struck he'd been. 'I watched like a desperate puppy from the sidelines. And when she came to me and said that they were done and that it was me she'd wanted all along… I didn't question her motives. It didn't occur to me that she would be disingenuous. That I was some pawn to make Carlos jealous.'

Luca shook his head. What a fool he'd been for

Marissa. What a stupid, naive fool. He glanced at Mia and marvelled at how little it suddenly seemed to matter.

'And then Marissa got pregnant and she told Carlos, who she apparently was still seeing, that the baby was mine. She told me it was his and the families came to loggerheads...' Luca shrugged. 'It was like the Capulets and the Montagues times one thousand.'

Mia couldn't really laugh at the joke. She could sense Luca was just skimming the surface and could only begin to imagine the repercussions.

'So who was the father?'

Luca shrugged. 'She miscarried and it became a moot point.'

'I'm sorry,' Mia murmured. 'That must have been hard for you. Losing a baby at any stage is difficult.' She'd been ten when her brand-new baby sister had been stillborn and that had been truly awful. 'And you were so young.'

Luca was momentarily taken aback. His family had been too angry at the time to acknowledge the emotional impact on him, let alone support him through it. Until today his grandmother had been the only person who had understood how much grief the incident had caused him.

He nodded then paused for a moment to pick up the thread of his story. 'A massive rift developed between the two families and it was only Marissa and Carlos's engagement that kept them together. I became the scapegoat.'

Mia felt his pain right down to her toes. And finally she understood his compassion with Stan that first night, a man who'd loved a woman that hadn't been faithful.

'But…surely your parents, your sisters…? They're your family…they're supposed to love you. No matter what.'

Even as she said it she felt a fraud—her parents had certainly forgotten all about what they were supposed to do, bogged down in the quagmire of their grief and anger.

Luca shook his head. 'Sicilians don't forgive very easily and I learned right then and there that love is no guarantee of anything. That any relationship, no matter how strong, can go toxic. I was sent to live with my grandmother in Palermo and as soon as I was out of school I left and didn't go back.'

'Until this week.'

Luca nodded. 'Until this week.'

'Was it hard…seeing them again? Your brother. And Marissa?' Luca shook his head. It had been a relief. Seeing Carlos and Marissa together no longer hurt. 'No.' Mia wished he'd elaborate. *Was he still in love with her?* But she shied from asking it, too frightened of the answer.

'Was there any mellowing?'

He shook his head. 'I was pretty much persona non grata.'

An almighty gust of wind seemed to shake the helicopter and her anger swirled inside the cabin with as much potency. 'That's not fair.'

Luca shrugged, looking out the window. 'Life's not fair. But I'm very pleased, very grateful to you, that I went. That I got to say my goodbye. Nonna anchored me during a very turbulent period in my life. To my shame, I don't think I appreciated that till many years later. I was angry for such a long time.'

Mia watched his brooding profile as he seemed transfixed by rain spatter patterns. 'I'm sure she knew.'

Luca nodded. 'I hope so.' He sat staring out at the inclement abyss for a moment before turning to her and saying, 'I've never told anybody this. I'm not really sure why I'm telling it to you.'

All he knew was how right it felt.

Mia gave a small smile. No matter what, she did not want to read too much into such an admission. People were never the same on holiday or just before plunging to their deaths in a helicopter.

It was practically an unwritten law. 'It's okay. Near-death experiences tend to encourage confidences.'

Luca chuckled. 'Maybe you're right.' He sobered before pinning her with a speculative stare. 'Your turn. What makes Dr Mia McKenzie tick?'

He knew there were things, deep-seated things, that made her the wonderful, non-cuddly woman he'd come to think of as naturally as he inhaled and exhaled.

It was Mia's turn to look out the window as his question made her squirm. She wasn't so sure she wanted a man who thought every relationship had potential for toxicity to know her deepest, darkest stuff.

'Same things as everyone else, I guess,' she hedged.

Luca watched her avoid his gaze. Right...so this wasn't going to come easy. But he was suddenly desperate to know what made her the woman she was. Why she didn't stay the night. Why she didn't cuddle.

Why she was looking anywhere but at him.

'Okay. Let's start with an easier question. Why did you become a doctor?'

Mia barely suppressed a snort. How could he know the answer to that question was about as entwined with her baggage as was possible? She glared at him. 'Why did you become a doctor?'

'A child nearly drowned in a lake near where my grandmother lived when I was a teenager. I helped revive her. I knew then and there I wanted to be a doctor.'

Of course. Trust Luca to have an answer. She only wished hers was as cut and dried.

Luca leaned forward in his chair, placing his elbows on his knees, and the foil crinkled. 'Come on, Mia. I told you mine.'

The beeps of the monitor seemed to mock her every thought. Oh, what the hell…

She glanced out the window again. 'My mother had a baby. A stillborn baby, when I was ten.'

Mia didn't want to be sucked back to that time but here, in the darkness, surrounded by the fury of mother nature, it seemed impossible not to be. 'One minute I was going to have a baby sister to dote on. The next minute she was gone. The doctors were so good. Kind and compassionate. Not just to Mum but to me too. I guess I made up my mind then.'

Luca watched her as she stared intently out the window as if the meaning of life was lurking in the treetops. 'That must have been a hard time in your life. Your parents must have been devastated.'

Mia snorted. 'You could say things were never quite the same again.'

Luca frowned. 'They didn't make it?'

Mia shook her head. 'My father walked out a few weeks later and found himself another family. My mother took to our couch and zoned out for the rest of my life. Last time I checked, she was still there.'

Things suddenly became much clearer for Luca. The

most important man in her life had deserted her at an age and during a time when she'd needed him most. And her mother had been too grief-stricken to fill the gap.

'I'm sorry,' he murmured. 'You were just a child. You didn't deserve to be abandoned like that.'

Mia could almost feel the intensity of her ten-year-old pain as she stared out the window. She rolled her head to look at him. 'I hated him for so long.'

Luca shrugged. 'But of course. You needed him and he wasn't there for you. Or your mother.'

Mia gave a harsh little laugh. 'My mother.' She shook her head. 'My mother let me believe that he was the bad guy. That he'd found a better family. But she lied to me for years.'

'Oh?' Luca frowned.

'I found my mother's file when I was a med student working at The Harbour. The baby wasn't my father's.'

Mia rolled her head back to face the window. The find had been cataclysmic and still sucked her breath away.

'I confronted her about it. She admitted that Dad walked out because he'd found out about the baby's paternity. She didn't defend herself or apologise for letting me think the worst of him. She just said that I didn't understand what it was like to be married to a man who worked twenty-four seven.'

Luca watched as a range of emotions flitted across her face. Her emotional fragility after the Stan incident suddenly tightened into crystalline focus. It must have stirred up all those old childhood hurts.

'Did you…did you contact your father…try and reconcile?'

Mia bit down on her lip—she would not cry. No matter how hard that particular part in the saga had been. No matter how polite and distant her father had been. He'd been hurt too deeply both by her mother and by her own refusal to have anything to do with him over the years.

'I did. But it was too late…the damage had been done. And he had three little children who adored him. Frankly, I was a painful memory that he'd put away in a box somewhere.'

The rawness in her voice caught him somewhere right in the middle. His solar plexus. *His heart?* His family's abandonment of him seemed to pale in comparison. At least he'd been older, more emotionally equipped to deal with it. 'I'm sorry. That can't have been a good time in your life. Especially when you were in the middle of your studies.'

Mia gave a little laugh. 'You could say I went off the rails for a while there. A lot of booze and partying. A lot of hooking up with men who I always thought wanted more but were only out for casual sex. Which led to more drinking.'

Ah, so that's what she'd been referring to when she'd told him she'd once liked alcohol a little too much. And maybe it also explained her reluctance to get involved in anything more than a one-nighter. Mia had taken firm control of her life.

'You did well to stop the spiral,' he commented. Mia nodded. Luca had chosen a good word. She *had* been spiralling. Into self-doubt and self-loathing. Each new man, each drink, had made her feel more and more sullied.

'I failed a major exam. Had to resit it. It scared me

silly. I suddenly realised that there was no point throwing away my future over a past I couldn't change.'

Luca nodded. 'Yes.' It was a lesson he'd had to learn too. 'It seems you and I have a lot in common.'

'Oh?' Mia quirked an eyebrow as she looked at him again. 'You got all boozy and floozy too?'

Luca chuckled. 'No. Well, no more than any other angry young man, I suppose. It took a while to realise that I couldn't change what had happened. To accept that my family were never going to take me back. But once I did, it sort of freed me a little.'

Mia studied his face. 'So that's it, you're totally Zen with the whole thing?'

Luca smiled. 'No, not totally. Let's just say I'm a work in progress.'

Mia's heart filled her chest as she smiled back. 'Guess that makes two of us.'

They smiled at each other for a moment then Brian groaned. Mia checked his pulses as Luca administered another small dose of morphine. And when they sat back down again they settled into a companionable silence, each caught in their own thoughts.

Mia yawned. 'We should get some sleep,' Luca suggested.

She nodded. She wasn't sure if it was the confession or the hour but she was suddenly bone-deep tired. And it seemed like the most natural thing in the world to shut her eyes as the man she loved shut his.

Mia wasn't sure what time it was when she woke. Or even what had woken her. But watery daylight lit the inside of the chopper and there was a strange buzzing, crackling noise that she didn't think was coming from the rustling of the space blanket.

She came fully awake as Luca leapt up, muttering, 'The radio.'

And then it was all stations go. No time to feel embarrassed about spilling all their private, closely held secrets in the dark or to analyse what opening up to each other meant. To work out where they stood. Or even to retract them.

No time at all.

The weather had settled and the rescue chopper was fifteen minutes out.

Forty-five minutes later, Mia was harnessed to a rescue officer, dangling over the drizzly treetops, looking down at a wrecked helicopter and a calm, solid Luca. Her eyes filled with tears as her heart swelled so large and full it felt like it was going to burst from her chest.

He was everything she'd ever realised she needed. But he'd only ever loved one woman. And maybe he still did. He certainly thought that all relationships had the potential to go toxic.

Just her luck that when she finally fell in love it would be with someone as damaged as herself.

Luca awoke with a start, vaulting upright. It was dark and he was momentarily disorientated. He'd been dreaming about Mia dangling over a dark, swirling, freezing mist. About her screaming his name as her hand slid from his and she fell.

His heart pounded like a freight train as he realised he was in his room. He glanced at the clock—six-thirty.

But was it morning or evening?

And what bloody day was it?

He flopped back against the mattress, taking deep breaths, forcing himself to calm down. It was just a dream.

A really bad dream.

Mia was safe. Brian was safe. They were all safe.

Mia…he'd lost track of her in the whirlwind that had descended on them the minute they'd set foot on the helipad at The Harbour. Whisked away for tests and debriefing and questions from all kinds of different official people and dozens of people dropping by to wish them well. When he'd finally been told he could go, there'd been no sign of Mia and Evie had told him that she'd taken Mia home and tucked her into bed.

His first instinct had been to go to her. But he'd checked it. She needed to sleep. Just because she'd opened up to him, didn't negate that they'd both been through a trauma and been up most of the night.

So he'd headed for his bed too. And despite his conviction that his speeding mind wouldn't allow him respite, the combination of the jet-lag and adrenaline had him out for the count within minutes of his head hitting the pillow.

But now he was awake. Wide awake. And he knew why. He knew why with every thud of fear still echoing in each heartbeat. He knew why he was dreaming about Mia. Why the overwhelming panic and despair at losing her—in the crash, in his dream—had woken him from deep and utter exhaustion.

He was in love with her.

He'd foolishly thought that they were just a casual thing. That they were having a bit of fun. Some great sex, a distracting flirtation.

But obviously his brain hadn't been listening.

Because while his body had been enjoying itself he hadn't realised his emotions had become involved. That their entire relationship had been based on a series of emotional connections—interlocking, weaving them together.

Stan and the emotional tumult of his case—for both of them—had been the first connection. Being held at knifepoint had been the catalyst for their initial sexual liaison. Sure, he'd dismissed it as a very nice, very surprising turn of events. But it hadn't been the uncomplicated one-off he'd been fooling himself it was.

It had occurred after a highly charged emotional incident.

And then later, when they'd worked together to save Stan's life, they'd forged an even deeper bond.

His grandmother's death had ramped it up a little more. Forced them to an even deeper level of emotional intimacy without him even knowing it. She'd been there to comfort him. To hold him. To tell him to get his butt on a plane and go to her funeral.

That had been more than just sex, no matter what she'd said.

For heaven's sake, she'd stayed the night. She never stayed the night. *She didn't even cuddle.*

And then there was last night. Sharing that near-death experience and then opening up to her, like he'd never done before. Unburdening all the ugly things about his past he never spoke about. Listening to her as she'd unburdened hers.

He'd been pretending it was casual. Having a great time with hard and fast sex, indulging in the physical to override anything deeper. But somewhere along the way it had become more than that.

For him anyway.

He loved her. And it didn't frighten him. He didn't want to run from it like he had in the past. Maybe returning to Sicily had laid some ghosts to rest. Maybe it was almost dying in that helicopter crash. Maybe it was *Mia* almost dying in that helicopter crash.

But he wanted to live. He wanted that grand love poets had written about. And he wanted it with Mia. His scarred, scared Mia.

He didn't want to live another day without it.

Mia woke to a terrible racket. She'd been so tired when Evie had finally dragged her home and pushed her into the shower, not even thoughts of Luca had been enough to keep her awake as she'd collapsed naked into bed.

It took her a moment to realise the racket was coming from the front door. 'Go away,' she groaned as she dragged the pillow over her head and shut her eyes again.

'Mia? Mia! Open up!'

Mia sat up as the voice registered. *Luca?*

'Mia!'

Luca's urgent tone penetrated the fog of fatigue. She was throwing back the covers and pulling on a robe before her sluggish brain even registered her purpose.

'Mia!'

'Coming!' she called as she hurried out of her bedroom, tying the robe firmly at her waist, half tripping over a discarded shoe on the way.

Why on earth was he pounding her door down? Her heart rat-a-tat-tatted in time to the knocks as it romanticised his presence. But she doubted he was knocking like a madman to tell her he loved her. More likely the building was on fire.

Which made her unaccountably grouchy.

She reached the door and snatched it open. Her breath caught in her throat. He stood before her in track pants and a hoodie, his feet stuffed into thongs, his hair rumpled, that stubble still peppering his jaw, a blanket mark reddening one cheekbone.

The man had never looked sexier.

'Where's the fire?' she snapped, because it was that or do something really silly like invite him into her bed.

She'd meant it when she'd told him they couldn't keep sleeping with each other. She couldn't love him and only have some of him. Know that he was waiting for the whole thing to go toxic.

Luca took in her tousled blonde hair and the outline of her breasts beneath her gown and smiled. 'You look good,' he murmured appreciatively.

Mia gripped the door at the lust she saw glittering in the deep brown depths of his eyes. 'I sure hope you didn't wake me for that.'

Luca smiled. 'Can I come in?'

'Luca,' she sighed. She was not going to be sucked in by that sexy smile.

'Please.' He spread his hands. 'Just for a moment.'

Mia almost shut the door on him. She was tired and at a really low ebb. Didn't he know she wanted nothing more than to curl up in bed with him and sleep for a hundred years?

Why didn't he just leave her alone?

Hoping she wouldn't regret it, she stood back and inhaled as he passed. She hadn't meant to but he smelled so good she let his aroma wrap around her like a warm cloak. She stood by the closed door, arms folded, as he strolled to the centre of her lounge room.

Luca turned to face her. She seemed remote. Both physically and emotionally.

That didn't bode well.

He took a step towards her. 'I figured out why I told you all that stuff last night.'

Mia regarded him warily. She hoped he hadn't figured out why she'd told him her stuff. The only way she could keep her dignity here was to hide her feelings. 'Really?'

He took another step. 'I've known somewhere deep inside for a while that you understood me, truly understood me, and I thought that it was just our family issues, our unhappy pasts uniting us in a way that few people could relate to.'

Mia nodded. She'd recognised him as a kindred spirit almost from the beginning.

'But it's more than that, Mia. You got under my skin, sneaked up on me when I wasn't looking. I was fooling myself that we were just keeping it casual but I was wrong.' He raked a hand through his already rumpled hair. 'I've been walking blindly down this track towards you all along and it's only now that I see what's really happening.'

Mia's heart started to thump erratically in her chest. What was he saying? That his toxicity sensors were twitching madly? That he was getting too close and it was time to get as far away as possible? 'Oh? And what's that?'

'I'm in love with you.'

Mia didn't say anything for a moment. She didn't

move. She didn't breathe. In fact, she was pretty certain her heart even stopped for a few beats.

'Mia?'

'What about Marissa?' she blurted out, because that was way simpler than the crash of other thoughts and emotions that were churning inside her.

'Marissa?'

'You said she was the only woman you ever loved.'

Luca frowned. 'I was sixteen. And infatuated. That wasn't love. I knew that the moment I saw her in the church in Palermo last week. I was a boy with a crush. What I feel for you…in here…' Luca patted his chest. 'It's a thousand times deeper, wider, stronger. You're the one I want to talk to, make love to, wake up to.'

Luca watched her face as she grappled with the news. She looked like she was fighting it. Trying to come up with ways to block it out. Block him out. He covered the distance between them until he was standing within touching distance.

'I know that you think you can't do this—have a relationship with someone. That it's not you. That you're not the *sleeping-over* type…'

'Me?' Mia scoffed, arms still firmly crossed. 'What about you? Aren't you afraid this will go toxic too? Because I'm not going to get involved with someone who's waiting for me to slip up or who's out the door at the first sign of trouble wearing a gas mask.'

Luca, buoyed by the concession that she might actually be thinking of getting involved with him, placed his hands on her shoulders and rubbed his thumbs against the polar fleece of the thick robe.

'I'm not saying that this doesn't scare me, that it's not new territory, but as you said last night I can't let an unhappy past, one that I can't change, ruin a chance at a happy future. Neither of us can, Mia.'

Mia felt tears well in her eyes. This couldn't possibly be true, could it? *Could he actually love her back?*

'Oh, Mia,' he murmured, drawing her against him. 'Don't cry, Mia. I love you.'

Mia shut her eyes tight as his accent washed over her like syrup and she allowed herself a moment to inhale the essence of him. Less than two months ago she hadn't even known this man. Just last night she'd realised the utter depth of her feelings for him. And realised he couldn't love her back.

Could she have been wrong?

'This is just the near-death experience talking.'

She tried to break out of his grasp but Luca held her tighter. Her voice was muffled against his shirt but he heard every word.

'No, Mia, no.' He eased her gently back. 'It may have been the jolt that removed the blinkers from my eyes, but this isn't sudden. I've known deep inside, deep in my heart since that night in the on-call room, that you were special. That you were more than just another woman.'

The sincerity in his eyes and in his husky accented voice called to her on a primal level. She laid her head back on his chest as she allowed the possibilities to bloom. 'I thought we were going to die last night and that I'd never get the chance to love you.'

Luca hugged her close as her words sang like an opera in his heart. 'You love me,' he said.

He'd hoped, he'd wondered, he'd wished. But to hear her say the words meant more than his next breath.

'I didn't want to,' Mia murmured.

Luca chuckled as he stroked her hair. 'Well, it's just as well we don't always get what we want.'

'Oh, Luca.' She pulled back and looked into his eyes, oozing love and joy. 'I love you so much, I couldn't bear anything to happen to us.'

Luca placed a finger across her mouth, shushing her, knowing what she was thinking. 'I'm not your father, Mia. And you are not Marissa. We're us and we won't make the same mistakes.'

And then he lowered his head and drifted the sweetest, softest kiss across her mouth she'd ever experienced. Her eyes fluttered closed and she sighed.

'Promise?' she murmured against his lips.

Luca chuckled. 'Promise.'

EPILOGUE

Two weeks later a limousine carrying Luca in a tuxedo and a glamorously dressed but blindfolded Mia glided to a halt outside the Sydney Opera House.

'We're here,' Luca announced.

Mia laughed. 'Luca, for the last time, where are we going?'

'Patience,' he teased, kissing her nose. 'Patience. Although we could just drive around in the back all night…' he dropped a kiss behind her ear '…and christen the seats…' His lips nuzzled her neck.

Mia laughed and pushed him away playfully. 'Oh, no. No way.'

The door opened and Luca grinned at the chauffeur. 'Okay, then, let's go.' He helped Mia out and once she was standing steadily he removed her blindfold.

Mia blinked as the illuminated sails of the Opera House filled her vision. She smiled at him. 'We're going to see a show?'

Luca smiled down at the woman he loved. 'The ballet, actually.'

Mia looked at the tickets he thrust into her hands. She read the fancy printing several times before it registered. She looked up at him, the man she loved, so tall and handsome and so, so hers.

'*Swan Lake*,' she whispered, hugging the tickets close. 'Oh, Luca…thank you.'

Mia beamed up at her Italian angel. She wasn't sure when she'd stopped seeing the devil but tonight all she could see was a pair of luminescent wings and a bright golden halo.

And he was all hers.

* * * * *

ROMANCE

Roccanti's Marriage Revenge	Lynne Graham
The Devil and Miss Jones	Kate Walker
Sheikh Without a Heart	Sandra Marton
Savas's Wildcat	Anne McAllister
The Argentinian's Solace	Susan Stephens
A Wicked Persuasion	Catherine George
Girl on a Diamond Pedestal	Maisey Yates
The Theotokis Inheritance	Susanne James
The Good, the Bad and the Wild	Heidi Rice
The Ex Who Hired Her	Kate Hardy
A Bride for the Island Prince	Rebecca Winters
Pregnant with the Prince's Child	Raye Morgan
The Nanny and the Boss's Twins	Barbara McMahon
Once a Cowboy...	Patricia Thayer
Mr Right at the Wrong Time	Nikki Logan
When Chocolate Is Not Enough...	Nina Harrington
Sydney Harbour Hospital: Luca's Bad Girl	Amy Andrews
Falling for the Sheikh She Shouldn't	Fiona McArthur

HISTORICAL

Untamed Rogue, Scandalous Mistress	Bronwyn Scott
Honourable Doctor, Improper Arrangement	Mary Nichols
The Earl Plays With Fire	Isabelle Goddard
His Border Bride	Blythe Gifford

MEDICAL

Dr Cinderella's Midnight Fling	Kate Hardy
Brought Together by Baby	Margaret McDonagh
The Firebrand Who Unlocked His Heart	Anne Fraser
One Month to Become a Mum	Louisa George

Mills & Boon® Large Print

March 2012

ROMANCE

The Power of Vasilii	Penny Jordan
The Real Rio D'Aquila	Sandra Marton
A Shameful Consequence	Carol Marinelli
A Dangerous Infatuation	Chantelle Shaw
How a Cowboy Stole Her Heart	Donna Alward
Tall, Dark, Texas Ranger	Patricia Thayer
The Boy is Back in Town	Nina Harrington
Just An Ordinary Girl?	Jackie Braun

HISTORICAL

The Lady Gambles	Carole Mortimer
Lady Rosabella's Ruse	Ann Lethbridge
The Viscount's Scandalous Return	Anne Ashley
The Viking's Touch	Joanna Fulford

MEDICAL

Cort Mason – Dr Delectable	Carol Marinelli
Survival Guide to Dating Your Boss	Fiona McArthur
Return of the Maverick	Sue MacKay
It Started with a Pregnancy	Scarlet Wilson
Italian Doctor, No Strings Attached	Kate Hardy
Miracle Times Two	Josie Metcalfe

Mills & Boon® Hardback
April 2012

ROMANCE

A Deal at the Altar	Lynne Graham
Return of the Moralis Wife	Jacqueline Baird
Gianni's Pride	Kim Lawrence
Undone by his Touch	Annie West
The Legend of de Marco	Abby Green
Stepping out of the Shadows	Robyn Donald
Deserving of his Diamonds?	Melanie Milburne
Girl Behind the Scandalous Reputation	Michelle Conder
Redemption of a Hollywood Starlet	Kimberly Lang
Cracking the Dating Code	Kelly Hunter
The Cattle King's Bride	Margaret Way
Inherited: Expectant Cinderella	Myrna Mackenzie
The Man Who Saw Her Beauty	Michelle Douglas
The Last Real Cowboy	Donna Alward
New York's Finest Rebel	Trish Wylie
The Fiancée Fiasco	Jackie Braun
Sydney Harbour Hospital: Tom's Redemption	Fiona Lowe
Summer With A French Surgeon	Margaret Barker

HISTORICAL

Dangerous Lord, Innocent Governess	Christine Merrill
Captured for the Captain's Pleasure	Ann Lethbridge
Brushed by Scandal	Gail Whitiker
Lord Libertine	Gail Ranstrom

MEDICAL

Georgie's Big Greek Wedding?	Emily Forbes
The Nurse's Not-So-Secret Scandal	Wendy S. Marcus
Dr Right All Along	Joanna Neil
Doctor on Her Doorstep	Annie Claydon

Mills & Boon® Large Print

April 2012

ROMANCE

Jewel in His Crown	Lynne Graham
The Man Every Woman Wants	Miranda Lee
Once a Ferrara Wife...	Sarah Morgan
Not Fit for a King?	Jane Porter
Snowbound with Her Hero	Rebecca Winters
Flirting with Italian	Liz Fielding
Firefighter Under the Mistletoe	Melissa McClone
The Tycoon Who Healed Her Heart	Melissa James

HISTORICAL

The Lady Forfeits	Carole Mortimer
Valiant Soldier, Beautiful Enemy	Diane Gaston
Winning the War Hero's Heart	Mary Nichols
Hostage Bride	Anne Herries

MEDICAL

Breaking Her No-Dates Rule	Emily Forbes
Waking Up With Dr Off-Limits	Amy Andrews
Tempted by Dr Daisy	Caroline Anderson
The Fiancée He Can't Forget	Caroline Anderson
A Cotswold Christmas Bride	Joanna Neil
All She Wants For Christmas	Annie Claydon

0312 GEN STD LP